PRAISE FOR NAOMI NASH!

CHLOE, QUEEN OF DENIAL

"Smooch is setting the mark in quality young adult fiction, with this being no exception."

—*Huntress Reviews*

"Beautifully written, life-like, and features characters that really pull you into the story."

—*Romance Reviews Today*

YOU ARE SO CURSED!

"This book perfectly describes an alienated teenager in the hostile environment of high school. This tale is perfect for library shelves."

—*KLIATT*

"How can you go wrong with a book about a faux witch, a hot guy, a poop-crazy goat and those girls you just love to hate?... This book finds a hilarious medium. Definitely recommended for the confused person in all of us."

—*RT BOOKclub*

"A marvelous book and a great addition to the Smooch line."

—*Romance Reviews Today*

"HARMLESS?"

It was the last word I expected. Or wanted. Eugene thought I was harmless?

"Yeah," he said. "You know, easy to talk to, not real threatening, someone I could be friends with. That kind of thing."

"The kind of girl you could talk to about other girls? The kind of girl you could tell about the movies you saw?" Eugene nodded. Was he an utter idiot? How could he say those hurtful things to my face and think they were kind? Now I knew what my sister felt like when she began one of her rampages. "What do I look like to you, some kind of *starter girl?* Do I have *training wheels* attached to my *behind* so you won't fall *off?*"

"I didn't mean—"

"You don't think I'm attractive at all? I'm not the kind of girl you'd mack down on?"

"You're getting it all wrong."

"So kiss me," I said. Even as I said the words, I knew I was out of control. What was I trying to prove with this? "Come on," I ordered him, pointing to my lips. "Plant one on me. I'll show you how *harmless* I am."

Other SMOOCH books by Naomi Nash:

CHLOE, QUEEN OF DENIAL
YOU ARE *SO* CURSED!

• BEANER O'BRIAN'S •
Absolutely Ginormous
GUIDEBOOK TO GUYS

Naomi Nash

SMOOCH NEW YORK CITY

SMOOCH ®

December 2004

Published by

Dorchester Publishing Co., Inc.
200 Madison Avenue
New York, NY 10016

ISBN 0-8439-5403-5

The name "SMOOCH" and its logo are trademarks of Dorchester
Publishing Co., Inc.

Printed in the United States of America.

ACKNOWLEDGMENTS

I am always indebted to Patty Woodwell for her keen eye and ability to hound me about my smallest errors, and to my critique partner Marthe Arends for her fabulous suggestions, and to Craig Symons, Michelle Grajkowski, and Kate Seaver for their encouragement and support. I must also express my gratitude to my wonderful friend Terry Danuser for his glimpses into the everyday life of a talent producer, and to the lovely Tahirah Shadforth for allowing me to appropriate her menus for the character of Jasmine. Special props, however, I owe to Andrew Wright, captain of the S.W.A.K. fan club, for his unnerving ability to instantly create and perform S.W.A.K. songs—and never a braver karaoke singer has this world seen!

· BEANER O'BRIAN'S ·

Absolutely Ginormous

GUIDEBOOK TO GUYS

CHAPTER ONE:

boy (n) 1: a young male person 2: a junior
version of the mature male, lacking the sophistication of the grown adult. As a species, they
are frequently prone to . . .

"Prone to what?" I asked. Usually I love the first blank page in a notebook, when it's still clean and white and waiting to be filled with thoughts. I'd only captured thirty words on paper, though. Two of them were the chapter heading. I was pretty sure they would not count. Four thousand, nine hundred and seventy to go, and word number thirty-one simply wasn't coming to mind.

I was in a world of hurt.

"To acne," said Taryn. She had been reading over my shoulder as I wrote.

I turned my head and gave her a dirty look. "Not. I was thinking about something like, *they are prone to blah blah blah, which as an adult manifests itself as yodee yodee yo.* I want to make this project sound as professional as possible."

1

Mandy lay on my bed, bouncing one of my pillows on the soles of her feet in time to the XT music channel. "Prone to believing unrealistic portrayals of female beauty, resulting in . . ." She had already started to giggle at our reactions to her unexpected wordiness. ". . . unsatisfying marriages and an increased divorce rate . . . *what?* My mother's a psychologist, hello!"

"Hel-*lo?*" Carrie echoed from where she sat at my desk. Lately Carrie doesn't like getting her outfits creased by lying on beds, or dirty from lying on the floor. I could never work out whether she was insulting my cleanliness or merely being quirky. "Not every boy is like that. They're not all constantly fantasizing about the girls of "Baywatch", Smut-derella."

"What's it about, then?"

For a minute, while Carrie gazed off into space, she seemed to lose touch with reality. If I'd been a movie director, I would have cued the dreamy music right then and zoomed in for a close-up. The camera would have caught the slight bite of her lip, the way her eyebrows rose in the middle, and even her unfocused expression as she considered the question. "It's about feeling you two are the only people in the world." Her eyes flicked back to Mandy, her eyebrows crashed down, and she tucked one corner of her lips into a scowl. "Not just sex and lust-aciousness."

"But there's sex involved, isn't there?"

Carrie returned to flipping through her fashion magazine with a flounce and a smirk. The silence meant that we weren't going to hear any dirty little details about her and Rick.

If I could direct my life on film, I'd have total control of how it came out. A minute ago with Carrie, at scene's end I would have yelled "Cut!" with her gazing off into space, wistful and tender. No one needed to hear Mandy turning the conversation back around to sex, the way she always did. Besides, if my life were a movie, I could do retakes. Wouldn't that be the coolest?

"Dictionary definitions aren't going to get your paper written, Beaner," Carrie told me. "If you want to write about boys, you need some experience. Before Rick . . ." I saw Mandy and Taryn roll their eyes and start a conversation of their own. Before Rick, Carrie had been totally silly like the rest of us. Maybe even sillier. Before Rick, whenever S.W.A.K. came on "XTreme Video Request" Carrie used to waffle over whether Scotty or Wyatt was cuter. Before Rick, Carrie had an absolutely huge poster of Justin Timberlake on the wall of her bedroom, not to mention a hundred photos of singers and actors and athletes cut from magazines.

After Rick, though, she'd ripped down every single one of those nummy, hunky guys and traded in *Us* and *People* for articles about how to make your tummy look trimmer. "Before Rick, you wouldn't *believe* the things I thought about boys. I thought they were rude. I thought they were disgusting and smelly. I thought they had nothing but sex on their minds."

We looked over to the bed, where Mandy was leaning over the edge to explain, ". . . told me that when guys reach a certain age, all the hair falls off the top of their head and starts to grow out of their ears, so they buy this paint that's kind of fuzzy and every morning they like, spray the bald parts so it *looks* hairy, but sometimes they leave fingerprints in it. . . ."

"Girl, you're *lying!*" Taryn screamed, laughing so hard that my bookcase rocked when she kicked her heels against it.

"If you two are *finished,*" Carrie announced in her no-nonsense tone. Although she was going to be a sophomore like us next year, Carrie is a year older and never lets us forget it. "When's this writing project due, Beaner?"

I looked down at the page. Word number thirty-one still wasn't getting written. "The first day we go back!" I gulped down my bitterness at the Lancashire School's requirement for creative projects over summer vacation. It was bad enough that three-quarters of the year I had to wear their tight, scratchy uniform. Summer was when I was supposed to enjoy myself! "Less than a month! I don't know how you guys got so lucky. You didn't have to spend your whole summer slaving over a stupid paper."

"You're the one who picked creative writing for your summer project," Taryn pointed out. "I have to do a photographic essay!"

"Big deal. Everyone in Miss Benson's class knows you load up some black-and-white film, head to Union Square Park, and take snapshots of homeless people."

Taryn gave me a scornful look. "I know you know that's not true, and I know you know I know, so just so you know, I'm giving you a break. We're not allowed to take photos of the homeless anymore, not since they found out about the kids who'd been giving a

4

homeless guy money to lie down in the gutter with an empty bottle and pretend he was unconscious."

"And I'm working on my watercolor portfolio," Carrie said, "And Mandy is . . . what are you doing again?"

"I finished already." Mandy reacted to our blank stares by abandoning the television, sitting up on the bed, and glaring back. "I was in that group violin recital at the little church in the Village last month. You were *there!* Don't you *remember?* God!"

"Oh, yeah," the rest of us murmured. Carrie had nearly fallen asleep in our pew that night, and Taryn and I had marked up the back pages of one of the hymnals with several games of Dots. We'd been there, all right, suffering through three hours of scratchy violin concertos and something called a rondo. It nearly had sent me rondo the bend.

Suddenly I felt a desperate need to scream. If only I'd started this stupid project weeks ago! "Thirty-three days until school starts," I said, stabbing at my calculator with my pencil. "That's only forty-seven thousand, five hundred and twenty minutes. I'll have to write over nine and a half words a minute at that rate, and I haven't written any in the last two!"

"Nine words a minute doesn't sound too bad," said Taryn. "That's only like, one word every seven seconds."

"I have to sleep *sometime!*" It came out sounding like a screech. "When am I supposed to have a life? I wish I played the stupid old violin."

"Hey!" Mandy protested. "I had to *practice!*"

A knock at my bedroom door interrupted our bick-

5

ering. When it swung open, Jasmine poked her face through the opening. Her skin was white and soft, like a glistening pearl. She must have spent the afternoon moisturizing again. "Hannah, do you mind if I come in?" The question was moot, since she was already standing in the middle of the room. Hannah. Ugh. I don't know which reeked more: my awful real name, or my worse nickname.

"Hello, Mrs. O'Brian," chorused my friends. I hated the way they all gazed at my stepmother with adoring eyes, like she was some fabulous movie star who had jetted in from Hollywood merely to say ta. Even Carrie had set aside her magazine to study Jasmine's outfit, memorizing her sleeveless white top and the long flowing pants that puddle on the floor around her impossibly long legs, and memorizing the long swoop of her jet-black hair and the shine of her long, expensive earrings. Yes, that ensemble was Jasmine's equivalent of wearing sweats around the house. In her hands my stepmother carried what looked like a piece of two-by-four.

Jasmine had the delicate laugh of a Walt Disney cartoon princess. You could almost picture little blue birdies alighting on her shoulders and squirrels and chipmunks running along carrying the hems of those elegant pants as she twirled and sang about what a chippy-dippy-yippy day it was. And then it would all crash down the minute she opened her mouth. "What's the dilly-o, yo? I do wish you girls would call me *Jasmine*," she corrected. "I've brought snacks for your . . . what do you homegirls say these days? When I was your age we called our get-togethers rap

6

sessions. Do you still say that? *Rap* sessions? No?"

I wanted to die. As if things weren't bad enough, her mouth kept flapping! "Are you *chillin* in your *crib,* hos? Word!"

Oh, God! When Jasmine asked the last question directly to Taryn, I actually wanted to commit matricide. It's hard to point a finger and accuse someone of prejudice, though, when you know she's only being her normal, totally-out-of-it self. Taryn didn't even seem to notice. She looked up at Jasmine with puppy-dog love in her eyes and said, "We're kinda hangin' out."

"Well! Hanging out. Isn't that the da bomb?" Jasmine knelt down and set the snacks on my little footstool. I could see now that it wasn't a two-by-four she'd been carrying, but a rough slab of wood that had been sanded smooth and varnished until shiny. "I've brought you a little French rustic afternoon *casse-croûte* for your 'hanging out.' Pacific wild sockeye smoked salmon, duck liver *pâté*, some St. Andre triple cream brie, Roquefort, some crusty baguettes, and mixed honeydew and strawberry topped with *crème fraîche.*"

With the exception of the old guy who grabs himself and says, "Hey, girlie! Hey, girlie! Hey, girlie!" to me every time I step on the subway, my stepmother is possibly the most *embarrassing* person in the world. "What in hell's so rustic about that?" I snapped, wishing she'd leave us alone already.

"Now, Hannah, I know you're at an age where you think it's the hot-diggety-dog to impress your friends with coarse language, but I don't think your father would appreciate it." Obviously my stepmother doesn't know my friends very well. They were probably more impressed I hadn't said worse. Jasmine's hands clasped her hips and she tilted her head to the side. For a woman obsessed with keeping her forehead wrinkle-free, that was as close as her expression got to annoyed. "And it's rustic because I've staged it on an antique plank I bought in the sweetest little boutique on Canal Street. It's originally from the Shanxi province of China," she added. I could see Carrie absolutely eating up that detail.

"Thank you, Jasmine," my traitorous friends said in unison.

"Later, homies!" she said, obviously pleased they'd used her first name.

I glared at the others until the only trace left of Jasmine was the scent of her expensive perfume. "You guys are scum."

"She's so beautiful," said Mandy, sighing, before she flopped back over to see what was happening on the XT.

"She's twelve years younger than my dad."

"She's so glamorous," Taryn said.

"She's twelve years younger than my dad!"

"I so want to be her." Carrie munched on a little slice of Pacific cross-eyed salmon as she stared at the closed bedroom door.

I sat back down on the floor. Much as I hated to admit it, the strawberries looked awfully good. "Didn't you hear how she *totally* insulted Taryn?"

Taryn was too busy figuring out the brie to reply. "Oh, she was joking around," said Mandy. "I wish my mom was funny and beautiful."

8

"I didn't notice any insults," Taryn said, finally using a strawberry to push some of the soft cheese onto a piece of bread. She sniffed at it and made a face before taking an experimental nibble. "I think Jasmine's great."

"Yeah? Well, you don't have to live with the tragic consequences of *your* dad's sad little midlife crisis, or Jasmine's artistic gay friends, or her Japanese expressionistic paintings, or her stupid Chinese floorboards." Taryn stopped eating. I heard Carrie breathe in sharply. Mandy's eyes bulged at a spot over my head.

"Hannah." I heard a voice from above and behind me. When I craned my neck around, Jasmine stood in the door once more. My insides suddenly felt as if a giant clammy hand had reached in and given them a good wash-day wring. How much of that had she heard? Writing programs came with an UNDO command. Why wasn't there one for my life? "I wanted to remind you we've rescheduled your final bridesmaid's dress fitting for tomorrow. Please don't disappoint your sister. Again. I'll leave you to your hanging now." Once more she let the door slip closed behind her.

Jasmine's cameo appearance felt like a slap in the face. Totally on purpose I'd hid out at Dad's office and skipped my scheduled appointment the week before. I don't know why, but when I don't want to do something, I curl up in a ball and hope that it goes away. It never does. When I uncurl, the thing I'm dreading's always still waiting for me.

"What color is the gown?" Carrie immediately wanted to know.

"Pillow mint," I said, heaping another indignity onto my already hefty pile. "Molly picked out a color called *pillow mint*. It's worse than awful."

"What color is pillow mint?"

"Lime sherbet green, only more nauseating."

"What kind of sleeves?"

"Puffy." I held out my hands wide, cupped into a circle, to show her. "The skirt poufs out at the bottom."

"I want a photo," cackled Taryn.

Photos? I had forgotten weddings always had photographers! Oh, man! Only three weeks until I'd be in a pillow mint bridesmaid's dress being photographed, when I already had a project to write and now a stepmother I'd have to be extra nice to because she'd probably heard me open my big fat mouth to speak my mind about her. Three weeks until I was stuffed into a hideous gown that made me look like a demented bag lady and stood up in front of God and the congregation of St. Blaise so my sister could become Mrs. Anas Aloul.

Honestly, sometimes I thought that Molly had only made me a bridesmaid so she'd look all the prettier in comparison. "That poor plain girl with that awful frizzy hair," I could imagine people whispering. "Who is she? The sister? You must be *joking*. But Molly's so pretty! And the mother, wasn't she once a model? Oh, *step*mother? You'd never know that little mouse was an O'Brian, looking at Jasmine and the bride. So lovely!"

That was me, plain old Hannah. Hannah the pal. Beaner O'Brian. If my plain face didn't turn you off, my baby nickname sure would. When I looked up, I caught Taryn regarding me with an odd expression. "Your face was twitching," she explained.

Of course it was twitching. I was about to have a good old-fashioned, stress-induced freak-out.

As if reading my mind, Carrie put down her magazine and pronounced, "Beaner's got too much on her plate, that's all." Who was she, my high school counselor?

"She's got a month until her project's due!" Mandy pointed out. "That's nothing to get stressed out over."

"But the wedding's in three weeks," Taryn said. "She's got all that running around to do."

"She should've started her project earlier, then. She's known about the wedding for ages."

"I *am* in the room, right?" I asked, tired of being referred to in the third person. "I didn't suddenly vanish? Hello? Can anyone see me sitting here, about to require therapy?"

Carrie's voice was unusually gentle when she reached down and took away my notebook. "Listen, smarty-pants, you're blowing everything all out of proportion." She ripped out the first page, crumpled it up, and tossed it in the wastebasket.

I wanted to bawl. "Those were thirty perfectly good words!"

She handed back my notebook. "What assignment did you take? Writing something about the opposite sex, wasn't it?" I nodded. Why had I thought it would be so easy when I saw the list of topics on Mr. Greenwald's bulletin board? What did Hannah O'Brian know about the opposite sex? I'd never dated like Mandy or Carrie. Boys liked me, sure, but only as a friend. I was the boys' gal pal, the girl they could joke around with, tell entire movie plots to, or play soccer with in Central Park. What in the world did I have to say about the opposite sex?

More to the point, in the looks department I wasn't anything like my older sister Molly. I wasn't a Carrie. I certainly wasn't a Jasmine—but who was? I was only a subordinary person with an insane stepmother, a father who thought I was still ten, a lunatic sister driving me nuts over her wedding, and a stupid paper due the day I got back to the Lancashire School in September.

"Summer projects are supposed to be fun. So enjoy it! Write about how girls can catch a guy quick and easy, a kind of 'Sex and the City' thing. Here. Take dictation." Carrie cleared her throat. "*A Guidebook to Guys* by Hannah O'Brian.*" She had to be kidding me. My chances of meeting a hot guy in a month, much less catching him, were absolutely zilch.

"*Hannah O'Brian's Guidebook to Guys,*" said Taryn, laughing. "That makes her sound like an expert."

"No one calls her Hannah, though. *Beaner O'Brian's Guidebook to Guys,*" said Mandy, bouncing my pillow off the wall.

"Oh, yeah, I can really see her handing that in," said Carrie. "*Beaner O'Brian's Big Book of Boys.*"

"You know," I repeated, feeling the sting, "I *am* here in the room with you freaks."

"Hah!" said Mandy, flopping over and sitting up. "*Beaner O'Brian's Absolutely Ginormous Guidebook to Guys!*"

"*Ginormous* is so not a word, Mandy-pants," said Carrie.

"It is too. It's *gigantic* and *enormous* all in one. Oh! It's on!" She flopped over to the other side of my bed and turned up the volume on the television until we could all hear the familiar opening music to "XTreme Video Request."

"You act like you're twelve, not fifteen," I told Mandy. "You don't see Carrie peeing her pants because the show's on." Carrie had picked up her magazine again and was pretending to flip through it in a bored manner, but over the top of the pages she would now and again flick a glance at my little TV. It's funny—for years we had watched this show together, and although we all were still glued to the set whenever it came on, we'd somehow reached a point where we pretended we didn't care about it. Mandy was the only one honest enough to admit she still loved the show. Why was that?

Taryn had joined Mandy on the bed, where they both sat with crossed legs as Aaron Grady's face filled the screen. For the top VJ on the most popular show on the XT, Aaron Grady sure managed to look bored all the time. "We're comin' at ya live from Times Square," he said, while a bunch of kids in the studio audience whooped and hollered from the pillows and rugs around the floor, "with your five favorite, hottest, and sexiest video picks of the day!" Massive cheering. "We got two today from one of the hottest bands out there, and they're kickin' it off with number five. Down one from number four yesterday, it's S.W.A.K., bringing it at ya from their latest release, *Party on the S Dub. . . .* "

"It's 'Fly Tonight'!" Mandy said, bouncing on the bed. "I think Scotty looks so *fine* in this video."

"He does look *faaaaahn!*" said Taryn, teasing her.

"Faaaaaaaahn!" Mandy agreed, then started singing along. " 'Flyyyyyyy! Flyyyyyyy! We're gonna fly tonight, it's gonna be all right!' " Her soft, timid voice harmonized with the S.W.A.K. boys on the a cappella section of the song before the beat kicked in.

I really wasn't in the mood for our usual "XTreme Video Request" ritual. Maybe my friends had been right. Instead of late July, I should have started the project when we got out of school. It's not as if I hadn't known about Molly's wedding. The ceremony was all I'd heard about for an entire year. Flowers blah blah, reception blah blah, place settings blah, photographer blah blah, shoes blah freakin' blah to infinity and beyond.

I suppose I hoped this project was one of those things that would disappear if I closed my eyes long enough. The only thing that had vanished, though, were my thirty original words. I was back to square zero. While the others watched the TV or, in Carrie's case, pretended not to, I took my notebook and went to sit in the window seat, where I could look out at the city.

Even when I was in the worst of moods, which lately seemed all the time, I loved gazing out at the city skyline. I couldn't see anything more than the immense—Mandy might have called them *ginormous*—high-rises that loomed over our smaller apartment building, and the sliver of green that was the park way down at the end of the street. At night, though, I could sometimes peek into the other windows and see other lives going on, and forget a little about my own.

Maybe I'd been doing a little too much forgetting lately.

A guidebook, hmmm? I might be able to handle that. While the others hummed and sang their way through videos from S.W.A.K. and Sistas on the Verge and Tossing Guppies, I stared at the blank page and willed the words to come.

Half an hour later, S.W.A.K. was back again with the video chart topper and I'd still written nothing.

"Huffin' and a puffin' thought you'd *blow* my house down, girl, you didn't guess it but I knew you was a clown . . . You thought I was a suckah but I knew you was a freak, girl, I couldn't help myself, we met when I was weak," Mandy declared in time with Kendrick.

Taryn stared at her. "White Jewish girls really should not rap. Like, ever."

I sighed. Okay. Fine. I'd moped enough. I had forty-seven thousand, four hundred and ninety minutes to write a project that sure wasn't writing itself. A guide-book could be a good idea. I mean, who better to write one than a person who really needed it the most? I could give girls like me a fun account of the differences between the sexes. I could catch myself a *faaaahn* boy and write about how I got him.

Where could I catch myself a few cool and cute guys, though?

"There he is," Taryn called out, pointing at the television as the "XTreme Video Request" credits rolled over the last of S.W.A.K.'s "When I Was Weak." I looked up at the screen. "There's your dad!"

XT Talent Producer . . . . Barry O'Brian

Our ritual ran the same each day—I could even pre-dict what was coming next out of Mandy's mouth. "Beaner, when is your dad going to get us in the XT audience?" Gack. Same question every afternoon, five days a week.

Mandy had given me an idea, though. Where could I meet a lot of really cute guys? Why not at the most popular music video station on the planet? Maybe this boy-catching thing might prove easier than I'd thought.

CHAPTER ONE:

Boys! Boys! Boys! Wherever you go, there they are—the boys! They're in Central Park! They're in Yankee Stadium! Everywhere you look, there are hotties nearby, and they're all waiting to be pounced on and snatched up! If a girl's lucky, the first friendly words out of his mouth when she approaches will be

"Hell no! No! No! And then some!"

My dad slammed his hand down on the desk with such force that his little wind-up nun wearing boxing gloves flew into the air and landed on the floor. "Don't you get struck by lightning for that?" Taryn whispered to me as she knelt down, scooped up the plastic nun, and stuck it back on the desk.

My dad winked at her, but his friendly face vanished within moments. "Hell no!" he repeated, rubbing a hand over his shaved head and tugging at the collar of his bowling shirt. "We did *not* agree to supply a *Lord*

17

of the Rings pinball machine for your client's dressing room, so you can take that breach of contract crap and—! You listen here, lady! No—you listen to *me.* No. No. *You* listen to *me.* That bill for five grand from the hotel room—yeah, yeah, you heard right. The XT isn't paying for a rehab deadbeat who ruins a mini-bar and breaks all the furniture in—oo! Oo! Hold on a sec, Patty." He held the receiver in his hand. "Honey, step outside for a minute. I've gotta use some strong language here that God forbid shouldn't be heard by anyone under the age of thirty-five and maybe not even then without a signed note from their priest and their proctologist. Ay-yi-yi." He shooed us off again. "We'll talk in a sec, honey. Wait outside."

The door had barely closed behind us with a thump when I heard Dad yelling again. Taryn followed me as I went back out to the waiting area and sat down with a sigh. I looked back at the door, where a shiny gold plate displayed Dad's name and title.

I think I liked it better when he worked for the Retirement Channel. I never saw him blowing a gasket over shuffleboard championships.

"I'm sure it won't be long." Fonzi, my dad's assistant, smiled from her desk. "He knows how to grab Patty Milhouse by the *cojones.*" She tapped one of her long nails against her teeth and went back to reviewing a file.

"Who's wrecked another hotel room?" Taryn asked her. I wanted to know, too.

"*Chicas,* what kind of confidential assistant would I be if I told you that up-and-coming rock star Julian Franklin and his girlfriend of the week had ruined an-

18

other suite at the Plaza? The kind whose fine little Latina butt your father would kick out that door, that's what kind." She didn't miss a beat or look up, but she did reach back with both hands and adjust her dark ponytail as she spoke. We both knew my father could never manage without Fonzi—she was so much a part of the family that she even spent every Thanksgiving and Christmas with us.

"Back in the day, the musicians I knew acted with respect," rumbled a deep voice. "Are you children out here again?" In the chair next to mine, Calvin put down the day's book, *The Rise and Fall of the Roman Empire.* Yesterday it had been *The Thorn Birds.*

"Yeah," I sighed. "Kicked out. Where did you and Dad go to lunch today?"

Calvin Desburne had been one of my dad's first clients, twenty years ago. He was an R&B singer with a string of hit singles who ran into alcohol problems, fired my dad, and kind of lost almost all his money. A real "Behind the Music" and "Whatever Happened To . . . ?" kind of guy. He and my dad are friends again, but all Calvin does these days is sit around Dad's office, read books, take lunch with him, and then head home to Queens at the end of the day. Calvin smiled at my question. "Your daddy and Calvin had take-out from that little Chinese place . . ."

"Thai," said Fonzi.

"From that little Chinese place on the corner . . ."

"Thai," Fonzi repeated.

"Good gracious God almighty, woman, let a man think his food is Chinese in peace! 'Tsah," he clucked, until Fonzi grinned at him and went back to her work.

19

"Oh," said Taryn from the chair on Calvin's other side. "I've got more stuff for you to autograph." She hauled out her backpack and began to dig through it.

"From your mama?" Calvin asked.

Taryn rolled her eyes and nodded. Mrs. Watson still had a serious hot pants explosion for Calvin Desburne. Calvin, however, looked pretty pleased when Fonzi tossed over a pen so he could sign the CDs Taryn dredged from the bottom of her bag. *Be My Lady Forever,* he sighed as he read off the title. "I didn't even think anyone bought that one. Mmm, mmm, mmm! And *By the Fireplace with Calvin Desburne,* the Japanese re-release, right? That's one I don't see that often. Thank heaven above for the folks of Japan, though—they're the only country where Calvin's still in print, and that's a fact if there ever was a fact." He pulled the insert from its plastic case and signed it with a flourish: *Girl, sit by the fireplace with me. Calvin Desburne.*

"Thanks!" Taryn said, taking a brief glance at his inscriptions before she tucked the CDs away.

I'd had an idea during the autograph signing. "Hey, Calv," I said, pulling out my notebook. "You know everything there is to know about, you know, falling in love, right?"

"Little lady, half the nineteen-year-olds across this country were made by young couples sharing a bottle of wine and listening to *By the Fireplace with Calvin Desburne.* I'd say Calvin knows something about the subject, all right."

"Well," I told him, liking my idea more, and more, "I have to write this project for school about the opposite sex, see, and—"

20

"Say no more." Calvin held up his big brown hand and grinned. Then he stroked the gray underside of his beard with the backs of his fingers. "Let Calvin see what you got."

I handed over the notebook. He was going to love this zesty start, I was sure. It was fun! It was zippy! It had life!

It didn't take him very long to get through the fifty-one words I'd managed to compose on the subway. Calvin looked at me, looked at the page, looked at me again, looked at the page again, and finally sighed. "Girl," he said, wrinkling his nose like I was wearing a perfume with a sardine base, "you've got to be kidding."

"What?" I was honestly baffled.

"That ain't no kind of romance!"

"What do you mean?" I'd expected Calvin to give me a big grin and tell me I was on the right track, and here he was acting like I'd sent him a bouquet of dead flowers and a card that said, *P.S., I always liked Luther Vandross better.* "It's supposed to be a handbook on how to win a guy."

"A *handbook?*" he said in total amazement. "A girl don't need no handbook to win a boy. The only book you need is the book of love." Even when he was talking instead of singing, Calvin had a habit of drawling the word like it was something kinda sexy and maybe a little bit dirty. *Loooooove.* He must've caught me rolling my eyes a little, though, because he kept talking. "Listen good, 'cause people used to slap down hard-earned money to listen to what Calvin knows about *loooove.* A man doesn't want his lady to pounce on him. He's not

21

looking to be snatched up like it's Thanksgiving dinner and he's the drumstick." The outside door to my dad's suite opened slightly as someone twisted the knob, letting in the sound of voices from the hallway.

"But on television the boys always go for the aggressive types. You know, the ones who see what they want and grab it." Nobody likes a wallflower, right?

"I don't know what trash you've been watching, but Calvin's gonna tell you something about men." He looked me dead in the eye and pointed a finger at me. "I don't care what their age or what their color, but the male sex wants a little *mystery* in the oldest chase of all. He wants a woman who'll make a little magic of her own with her hair and her face and what she wears. And when it comes to the capture, he wants to be the hunter. He wants to view his lady, he wants to woo his lady, so he can pursue his lady, 'cause she's the only one who'll ever do, his lady. He wants to choose her, 'cause he'll never refuse her, and when he woos her, he'll never *ever* abuse her. Because she's his lady."

There had been a certain rhythm to his explanation that made me suspicious. "Are you going to start singing?" I asked him. Over at her desk, Fonzi listened with a fascinated expression. She quickly put her head down when she saw me look her way. Calvin gave me a pained expression. " 'Cause you look like you're going to start singing, that's all. Okay. So you're saying that if a girl is into a guy, she ought to—" I poised my pen to take notes, because it looked like I was going to have to start over on my guidebook. Again! For a moment I was distracted, because on Calvin's other side, Taryn was busily fixing her hair. "What happened

22

to your glasses?" I asked her. Her wire-rims had totally disappeared.

Taryn squinted in our direction. "I took them off for a minute. That's all."

"Why?" Taryn was blind as a bat without her glasses.

"They were hurting my ears." I narrowed my eyes as she quickly plucked out a wand of gloss from her bag and ran the gooey tip over her lips. Acting on a hunch, I looked over my shoulder. Sure enough, two interns were standing out in the hallway. Hamilton Browder and Faris Aloul hung onto the doorknob, listening to one of the XT suits tell them something about setting up chairs in one of the studios. Taryn hesitated, put on an extra layer of lip gloss, and put the wand away. Her lips were now so shiny that if she and I were ever the only two survivors in a plane crash over the desert, I could have reflected them in the sun to signal planes passing overhead.

" 'They were hurting my ears,' " I mimicked. "Liar. You're all about Hamilton."

"Well, he sure doesn't hurt my *eyes*," she admitted, standing up for a second to smooth down her shorts.

"Not if you can't see him, he won't. Anyway, he's not your type," I said for the twelve-hundredth time that summer. I should've figured the prospect of seeing Hamilton was what made her ask me if she could come visiting with me.

"Why's he not my type, because he's a white boy and I'm young, booty-liciously gifted, and black?"

She knew that wasn't at all what I meant. "No, because Ken dolls are less plastic than him. That's why."

"Whatever. He looks *faaaaahn* to me. How about

me?" She adjusted the lay of her top and raised her eyebrows. I nodded. She looked good.

"Now this is what Calvin's talking about, little lady. Miss Watson here is a woman who is ready to be chased." Calvin raised his eyebrow at me as if he'd made a point. Maybe he did have one—Taryn might not have settled on a steady boyfriend yet, but she'd never had any problems attracting offers to upperclassmen dances, while the closest I ever got to a date was hearing boys tell me what other girl they planned to ask out.

Being every boy's confidante isn't the same as being an object of desire. It's not even a good consolation prize. Why was I so unlucky? Attractiveness couldn't only be about clothes, because at the Lancashire School, all the girls wore the same uniform. We were all on the same level playing field nine months out of the year. It wasn't solely about the way we did our hair or to what crowds we belonged. Okay, some of it might have been about the amount of frontal real estate pushing out our white blouses, because some boys are all about that. But I had as much in that department as Taryn, though less than Mandy and certainly more than Carrie, and they were way more successful than I at getting attention. If you stood the four of us in a lineup and paraded us in front of a bunch of guys, the three of them would be showered with offers for movies and concerts, while the shyer boys would quietly be asking me, "You know her? You think she might be into me?"

When Hamilton finally came into the room, he looked around and smiled before ambling over to Fonzi. It was one of those smiles that guys flash around

24

when they know they're attractive and can afford to be generous—meaningless but friendly. I heard Taryn heave a breath. She really had something for him.

It was hard not to, I had to admit. Hamilton Browder had the thick hair of a surfer dude, darker at the roots but sun-bleached at their blond ends. He was tall and blue-eyed and broad-shouldered, had perfect teeth, and looked like he'd seconds before stepped out of some acne medicine ad. The clean-complexioned "after" part, of course. Even his dark eyebrows looked as if they'd been professionally shaped. What other boy has perfect eyebrows?

"Beaner—just the broad I wanted to see!" Yikes! While I had been observing the object of Taryn's desire, Faris Aloul had zoomed over and stuck his face into mine. Talk about eyebrows! Faris's were all over the place. Every hair was dark and wiry and stuck out at a different angle from the others, so that whenever he raised one I had an uncontrollable urge to use it to scrub out a nearby toilet. It's not that Faris was bad-looking, exactly. In fact, because of his olive skin and dark hair, a few girls might consider him pretty delish. When Hamilton was in the room, though, everyone's attention was on him—no matter who else might wander in, from movie star to FBI ten most wanted. Plus it's hard to take Faris seriously after he tried to unhook my bra through my blouse the first time he met me last year. "Dude, did you see *Hellrush II: All Soul's Eve* yet? Awesome movie!"

That's all I was. One of the dudes. "Excuse me," said Taryn, smacking her lips and standing up. Stumbling a little, she blindly made her way over to Fonzi's desk,

25

where Hamilton stood. For a second, I watched her turn on the charm and speak to the nummier intern. Beside me, Calvin made a little grunt of amusement.

"Okay," said Faris, taking over her chair. He pulled up his legs by the cuffs of his blue jeans and tucked his feet under opposite knees. Like Hamilton, he had on one of the green XT T-shirts all the interns had to wear. Was he trying to grow a goatee? That was new. It looked a little like eczema. "So like, the Hellmaster had been buried under this like, total pile of cosmic mucus at the end of the first *Hellrush* movie, and then this law firm comes along and they've hired these burly dudes to un-bury him, right, because they're an *evil* law firm. . . ."

Over at Fonzi's desk, Taryn talked quietly to Hamilton, her head tilted to the side. I imitated her and cocked my own head. Was that a flirty thing? Would it work in the guidebook?

Unfortunately, Faris took the motion as a sign that I wanted to hear more about the movie. What is it with guys and movies and me? None of them wanted to *take* me to a movie, but they sure got off on spoiling them for me. "I know! It's wild! So they're an *evil* law firm, and then these mercenaries come and the music's all dum-dum-*dum* while they're chipping away at the mucus, and—"

"Don't you have something interny to do?" I asked him.

He stood up and walked around to perch on the arm of my chair. "Well, yeah, we've got a set-up this evening for a live set with Tossing Guppies, and then I'm kind of going to be hanging out with Aaron for a while. You know, Aaron Grady," he said, bobbing his head up and down in a way that said, *Yeah, I'm cool.*

I could see through the bluff. I knew all the slop-work the XT interns had to do, and it was nothing more than moving and stacking and undertaking grunt work no one else wanted. "Hanging out with him, as in standing on the other side of the studio while some junior flunky snaps her fingers and tells you to go get bottled water and Dentyne for the sound crew, hanging out?"

Instead of answering, he started plucking at my hair, lifting up a handful and dropping it back down again. Then another, and another after that. "That's really irritating," I told him. When he kept messing with me, I had to remind myself that I was a cool, calm, collected, almost–sixteen-year-old who did not haul off and pound people to the ground with her fists, no matter how much I wanted to. "*Quit* it," I snapped. Why did boys have to be so childish?

He only stopped when Taryn finally broke away from Hamilton and, with a smile on her lips, groped her way back across the room to me. "So?" I whispered. She gave Faris a dirty look. Oh. Naturally she wouldn't want to say anything in front of him. "Go away," I told him.

"Why?

"It doesn't matter why. *Go away.*" I rocked my chair from side to side, angry with him for making me snappish.

"Yeah, well, if you're going to be like that, I won't tell you who's coming to the studio later this week."

I leaned forward. "Fonzi?" I called out. She craned her neck to look at me. "Who's coming to the studio this week?"

She popped her gum. "Girl, do you know how dead your father would kill me if I told you that this week Mindy Moon and Chiarra and the Miami Boys are appearing? D-E-A-D dead, that's how dead." When my dad's buzzer sounded on her desk, she muttered, "I might be d-e-a-d now, in fact," and picked up the phone.

Faris's face fell. Could it be any more obvious he'd hoped I'd tease the information out of him? "Go away," I repeated.

Finally he stood up and took a few steps away from me. "You know, it was your dad I came to see anyway, not you."

"Fine. Go see him."

"Hey. I'm only trying to be your pal," he said.

That did it. I had more boy *pals* than I knew what to do with, and I sure didn't need another one who felt compelled to give me summaries of every movie he saw or video game he played. "Why?" I said. "You know, just because your brother is marrying my sister doesn't mean we have to be *pals*. In fact, we could see each other only at the wedding and never again and I'd be okay with it. Go get some doughnuts or whatever it is you do."

I shooed him off while Taryn took his place on my chair's arm. Honestly. You'd think he would have gotten the hint by now. Calvin shook his head as Faris rejoined Hamilton over by Fonzi's desk. Though his nose was deep in his book, Calvin had obviously paid attention to all that nonsense. "Lot of difference between a boy and a man," he said, his face sheltered by the Roman Empire.

"You're telling me," I agreed. I doubted Faris would ever be a mature adult. "So what happened?" I asked Taryn.

"I'm coming down here tomorrow and we're going to get some gyros." She tried to seem casual as she slipped her glasses back on. When she saw me raise my eyebrows, she held up a hand and smirked. "Oh, yes, oh, *yes*, it's true. Do *not* be hatin' just 'cause I'm datin'."

Calvin burst out into a laugh so hearty that it boomed around the office and made the book on his belly shake. "Now see," he said to me, "that's the kind of thing you need to be writing about."

For a minute I felt a burst of excitement. Maybe I could write about Taryn! "Wait a minute, though," I said, enthusiasm dampened. "You told me that guys like to woo a woman, pursue a woman, schmooze a woman, or whatever, and not be pounced on. But Taryn went over and devoured Hamilton like he was a Chicken McNuggets Super Meal and she was one of those wolves from *The Call of the Wild*. That's what I *was* writing about."

"Nah, she didn't."

"Yes, she did."

"Naaaaah, she didn't."

Taryn looked smug. "Oh, yes, I did."

We both stared at Calvin for a moment until he picked up his book again. "There are some things you children won't understand for a few years yet." I'd never seen him look so grumpy before.

Taryn and I didn't even have time to laugh before Fonzi waved us over. "Hey, *chicas,* you can go back in now, but I'd make it quick if I were you."

Dad was on the phone again when we slipped back through his door. At the sight of me he waved his fingers and signaled that I should sit down. "Yes, sweetie. Yes, she's here. Yes, I know she's your daughter too now, but . . ." he said into the phone. Instantly I figured Jasmine was on the other end. Of course, Dad might have had another sweetie, but as long as she was normal and didn't walk around the apartment with odd-colored facial goo spread all over her face, that would suit me just fine. "What?" He listened to her talk for a moment. "Yes, honey, I put a picture of Lake Placid on the front of my desk like you suggested, to ground my . . . *Bagua?* Is that like a crazy bagel? Yes, darling, I know how much feng shui has helped you. Yes, yes, I know that my spiritual life is important too—but honey, my spiritual life isn't paying for this weddi—love you too, darling. Buh-bye." He hung up the phone. "Oy."

"Okay, Dad, here's the thing," I told him. I'd worked up a big speech about how he should let me interview some guys around the XT. "I've got this summer project I'm supposed to be writing about the opposite sex, right? And I thought maybe you might let me come down here in the afternoons and I could—"

"No."

I felt a little taken aback when he looked me right in the eye and said that word, that one awful, forbidding word. At the Lancashire School, though, they're always encouraging us to develop our independence and self-empowerment, so I kept plowing on. "—and I could meet some—"

"No."

"—it's only that I was thinking—"

"No."

"Dad!"

"Honey. Baby. What have I told you about my job?"

"It's only that—"

"Your father's job is not glamorous. It is not filled with hanging out with Donny Osmond." Donny Osmond? Did he think that was a plus or a minus? Dad held up a hand before I could interrupt. "I don't go to cocktail parties all day. I'm not an executive producer. I'm the poor schmuck who gets plane tickets for other poor schmucks who've got pretty faces and who may or may not be able to sing and makes sure they're schlepped around and that they're on their spots when Aaron Grady picks up his mic and starts talking on air, that's who I am."

"But you could get me into the audience of 'XTreme Video Request.' Us, I mean." Taryn would never forgive me if I didn't include her. She sat still and listened with a hopeful expression on her face.

"I could. I could also dress you in fishnets and sell you on the Internet as a mail-order bride to some walrus-eating communist in Siberia, but no father in his right mind would do that either." He must have seen the bitter disappointment on my face, because his tone softened. "Sweetie, if you were older . . ."

How much older do you have to be before you're older? It was arguments like this that made me want to stamp my feet and pout and throw a temper tantrum like I used to when I was . . . well, eleven or twelve. But you know, when you keep trying to convince your dad to treat you like a grown up, it doesn't make sense to act like a little baby—even if every instinct in your body is telling you to. I took a deep breath and tried to play it cool. "Daddy, please? I'm only asking because . . ."

"No. Honey, that's final." One of those stamps escaped, and my lip poked out into a pout, but I manage to keep quiet my response of "That's not *fair!*" so I wouldn't get the whole life-isn't-fair-and-here's-a-zillion-reasons-why-you-should-get-used-to-it speech that I've been hearing ever since I was old enough to understand both English and the ways parents could turn it against me. "And furthermore, even if I was the kind of father who let his daughter dress up in a tight tube top and skirt so short that the boys could see her cookies, like some . . . some . . . some . . ."

He rubbed his face with both hands. "Skeezer?" Taryn supplied, trying to be helpful. "Skank?" I glared at her but kept my mouth shut. When Dad was on one of his verbal rampages, it was best to let him run with it.

"Yes, thank you, like some skeezy skanker, I *certainly* wouldn't let you do it until you had fulfilled *every familial obligation* that you had neglected and/or forgotten. Which fulfillment, young lady, you have not seen fit to discharge."

Yikes. You could always tell things were pretty serious with Dad when he began to talk like a producer. He stared at me, mouth closed, eyebrows raised, palms down on his desk. Obviously he expected me to

32

respond. After a couple of moments I couldn't stand it anymore. "What?" I had a nagging feeling at the back of my brain. Something kept trying to surface. I wasn't quite sure . . .

"Oh, crud," I said at last, flooded by guilt. I wished I'd never gotten out of bed that morning.

"Uh-huh!" said my dad, nodding.

"Bridesmaid's dress fitting?" He touched one index finger to the tip of his nose and pointed the other at me. I'd forgotten my appointment a *second* time. Molly was absolutely going to *kill* me. She'd probably decide I'd deliberately ignored it. For the rest of my life her revenge would be to nag me about my shortcomings. I knew Jasmine was probably having a fit back at home. My dad didn't look any too happy, either.

Why did I always screw these things up? "I'm sorry," I told Dad. "I won't forget next time, honest."

"Nuh-uh," he said, waving a finger. "You're not going to miss it *this* time. Do you know how much I am paying for this wedding? I am going into debt to the tune of eighty-f—don't you make that face, Hannah O'Brian! You might not think this is a serious conversation, young lady, but I can assure you I am *very* serious, and so is your sister. Faris, get in here."

I looked over my shoulder as Faris popped his head around the door frame. He'd obviously been eavesdropping. "Yes, sir?"

"You're taking my daughter to the Myra Chin Bridal Boutique on Madison. My assistant will give you cab fare. Make sure she gets there, stays there, and doesn't wander off."

"Um." Faris's expression might have appeared in

the dictionary to illustrate the word *dubious*. "She's kind of hard to control, sir. No disrespect intended."

"Ay-yi-yi. Listen up, Faris. I got you this internship, right?" Faris nodded. "I did it as a favor to my future son-in-law, your older brother, right?"

"Yes, sir."

"Then you can do this little thing for me. Let's make it fun for you. Internships should be fun. If she gives you lip . . . I don't know. You can cut off her finger with a paper knife."

"Dad!" I howled.

"Cool!" Faris said from the door. I heard Fonzi open her desk to dip into the petty cash box.

Hamilton stuck his head in as well. "Do you need me to go too, Mr. O'Brian?" he said in his deep, cultured voice. Taryn certainly seemed to approve of the idea. She quickly removed her glasses and smiled at him over her shoulder.

"No thanks, kiddo. I mean it, Beaner." Dad turned his attention to me once more. "Don't disobey me."

"But I'll never make it! The appointment's for four and it's ten 'til, now!"

"Oh-ho, *now* you remember your appointment times. Very convenient. Better get going, then. Chop-chop."

I looked at Taryn, my face wrinkled up like a pug's. We'd planned to go find some iced mochaccinos somewhere. She smiled in a child-tested-and-parent-approved way. "I don't mind going along. I'd *love* to see your *beautiful* and *expensive* new dress."

Ooooooo, I have evil friends. I decided to make one

34

last appeal. The thought of being rushed through traffic by some crazy cab driver over to Madison Avenue was really too much to handle right then. I just wanted the quiet afternoon we'd planned. You know, alone out in the middle of a city of eight million people. Was that too much to ask? "Dad—" I started to say.

He was already on the phone again. "This is Barry O'Brian at the XT," he said, waving us away with one of his hands. I shrugged at Taryn and we turned to leave. In the doorway, Faris was grinning at me like he'd won a Christmas turkey at bingo. "Yeah, get me Marty Dallin, if you would. I've got Antonio and Kendrick due in any minute at LaGuardia and they've got this weird thing in the contract about an SUV limo. Yeah, I know. I want to find out if a Hummer limo's acceptable. Yeah, I'll hold. Sheesh. Hummer limos," he muttered to himself.

When I was a kid we used to play something called freeze tag, where if the person who was *it* touched you, you had to stand as still as a statue. Taryn and I froze like we'd been tagged in the middle of my dad's sentence. You could've spray-painted us white and displayed us as statues at the Met. While Dad waited on hold, grumbling and shuffling through some contracts on his desk, we both slowly thawed and turned around.

"Antonio?" I asked. "Kendrick?"

"Yeah," said my dad. He looked up and saw our wide-eyed, awed expressions. "Uh-oh."

"Dad, you *have* to let us meet them! It's Antonio and Kendrick!"

"Oh, please, Mr. O'Brian!" Taryn begged. Any of

the sophisticated cool points she might have scored earlier in the afternoon by making a date for gyros with a certified surfer god, she lost by squeezing her knees together and jumping up and down like a little girl who had to pee. "We *love* them!"

"Antonio and *Kendrick!*" I yelled.

I might have squealed at that point. Taryn told me I did. I'm not sure I choose to believe the word of someone who screeched "S! W! A! K!" in time with every bounce.

"Oh, Daddy, I've never asked you for *anything* before." On seeing his expression I amended it to, "I've never asked you for *much* of anything. Nothing *important*. But S.W.A.K. is our favorite, favorite, *favorite* . . ."

"No."

"Oh, *please!*"

"You were the one who told me two weeks ago that boy bands were out, were you not?"

Curses! Why did I have to be sophisticated two weeks ago? Next time I accuse my dad of never listening to me, I hope someone reminds me of this conversation. "I was in a mood, then," I backtracked.

"Well, you got me in a mood now. My answer's still no. Yeah! I'm here." Dad glared at me as he returned to his phone conversation. "The Hummer works? Great. That's all we got here, anyway." He held his hand to the receiver and hissed, "*Faris! Get them out of here!* Yeah, yeah, we're doing great here, how's everything at your end?" he said in his normal tone, then covered the phone again. "*Take the paper knife with you!*"

If there's anything I've learned from fifteen years of

intensive study of my father, it's that you can push him only so far. Although every atom of my body wanted to stay and argue with him, I knew that if I did, I might find myself grounded without privileges until the age of thirty-seven. It was bad enough he was already fuming over my nearly missed dress fitting. One more word and that walrus-eating Siberian communist was going to start looking pretty good.

"What's that Kendrick guy got that I don't?" Faris wanted to know when we trudged into the office. At least Fonzi and Calvin were kind enough to pretend not to be listening.

"Brains. Looks. Personality. Fame. Money." I ticked off my thumb and fingers. "Want me to go on?"

"Your dad said I could cut off your finger if you got out of line," he reminded me.

I shoved him roughly in the direction of the office door. "If you try it," I told him, my teeth gritted, "you will find that paper knife shoved so far up your rear end that you will need a telescope and a pair of barbecue tongs to retrieve it."

"*Hey hey hey!*" I heard from the rear office. "*Am I the kind of man who would teach his daughter to use that kind of language?*"

There was a pause. Then Calvin and Fonzi both called back, at precisely the same instant, "*Yes!*"

If I hadn't been in such a foul mood, I would have actually kind of enjoyed that moment.

CHAPTER ONE:

She's sleek as a fox. She's wily as a coyote. She's today's young woman, and she's a wild creature of mystery as she

"Looks like you're startin' your own harem back there, kid. So what country you from, anyway?" asked the cab driver, peering in the rearview mirror at the three of us crammed into the backseat. He'd already been chattering for ten minutes about bad traffic. How could I be expected to concentrate? I tilted my notebook so that Faris couldn't see what I wrote.

"America." Faris kept beating some imaginary rock rhythm on the back of the seat with his hands. Freak. The cab stunk. I couldn't imagine voluntarily touching any of its filthy surfaces.

she's a wild creature of mystery as she prepares for the hunt . . . the hunt of

"Nah, buddy. I mean, like, where are you from? Iran? Iraq? Egypt? Whaddaya call it, Pakistan? Kuwait?" The driver slammed his ham-sized fist onto the horn as we screeched to a stop. "Get outta the friggin' road, you big so-and-so! Anyways, what kind of Arab are you?"

Taryn sighed, pulled down her skirt, and looked out the window as if she was contemplating ducking out of the door and taking the train back home. Squeezed between us, Faris had gone uncharacteristically silent. He'd stopped his drumming, put his hands back into his lap, and seemed somehow to have curled into himself. He made a face like he'd sucked on a lemon slice, then very quietly said, "I'm an American."

the hunt of love, where the hunter can be captured by his game. When

"Okay, yeah, yeah, but where did your folks come from?" asked the driver. "You feel safer around some Arabs than others, know what I mean?"

I'd never seen Faris look so surly, not even the time a couple of weeks before when I'd threatened to post on the intern bulletin board a bare-butt baby photo that I'd snitched from his brother's wallet of Faris on an honest-to-God bearskin rug. "They came from Queens."

When she

"But where—"
"Oh, for the love of Pete," I exclaimed. I was never

39

going to get any work done! I looked at the driver's badge as the traffic light finally changed and we turned onto Madison Avenue. "Listen, Mr. Przbylow-icz." That name was harder to kludge through than I expected. "My family came to Manhattan from Ireland on some boat eons ago. My other friend's family came over on some boat, not willingly, from Africa. Your family came over on some boat from what, Poland? And if this guy's family came here from Jordan, which is a country and not only a basketball player, then it really doesn't matter. We're all here now, right?" Faris had crossed his arms during my speech and turned his head away. "So are we *there* yet?" After fifteen minutes of the cab driver's obnoxious questions, I never wanted so badly to be at a bridal boutique in my life.

Wrong thing to say. I'd ticked him off. "Myra Chin," announced the driver, slamming on his brakes so hard that we all nearly banged our skulls on the greasy leatherette of his front seat.

"Have a *nice* day," said Taryn to the driver after we'd stepped out onto the curb. Faris had stuffed a few bills into his hand. "Buh-bye." Scarcely had Przby-lowicz pulled away from the curb than she wailed, "Oh, no! Did I leave my bag in that awful car?"

"I don't remember you having it," I told her after a moment's panic. The taxi had already vanished among the other yellow cabs. Even if we did give chase, we'd have to pick it out from the dozens honking their way up and down the crowded street.

"She didn't." What kind of boy notices whether or not a girl's got her bag? When I stared at Faris, he spread open his hands. "I was the one you two kept banging against all the way over here," he complained. "Trust me, I know every buckle, bag, and sharp object you were carrying."

Taryn still bit her lip and peered after the obnoxious driver, wherever he was. "I don't think it was in the cab. You probably left it in my dad's office," I told her. "We can head back over to the XT to pick it up after we're done here."

Boy, that Przbylowicz guy hadn't done us any favors by dropping us off an entire block away from the Myra Chin boutique. It was getting close to rush hour, and it seemed like everyone was streaming toward us. I enjoyed struggling against the crowd, though—it was a little like walking against a strong Hudson River wind on a cold day. You took a deep breath, braced yourself, and leaned into it, hoping for the best.

The first thing I noticed when I walked into the Myra Chin Bridal Boutique was the aroma. Madison Avenue in the summer is a rank stench of people and tobacco and hot cement and diesel, but after we stepped through the shop's tall, dark wood doors— the kind you expect to see on English manor houses— it smelled like we'd walked into some kind of green valley covered with bluebells and lilies and wild roses. Real Turkish carpets lined the wood floor and huge sprays of fancy flowers decorated the antique wood tables. Once the doors closed behind us, the place was quiet, quiet, quiet, except for classical music playing in the background. I assumed the music came from a loudspeaker, but I wouldn't have been surprised to see a real string quartet at the other end of the lobby.

The whole thing was like walking from a movie set for a gritty New York police drama into a "Masterpiece Theatre" production. Taryn looked as if she'd stepped through the pearly gates and into Heaven's waiting room. She gazed around with wide eyes and whispered, "I'd sell my soul to get my wedding dress from here."

"I'll marry you," said Faris, speaking up for the first time since the cab.

"I'd sooner be one of those spinster ladies who collects eight-foot stacks of old newspapers and lives with thirty-two cats," Taryn replied, still gaping. "Oh, my God. Are those chocolate truffles?"

The three of us had just swooped down like hungry vultures on the crystal bowl of chocolates when a middle-aged woman with a smart haircut, a dark suit, and a clipboard appeared from nowhere. "Miss O'Brian?" she asked. At Taryn's shove, I tripped forward. All the wonder I'd felt at the overwhelming room vanished in a flash when I realized I was supposed to be here for a reason. As if reading my mind, the woman gave me a sympathetic, private smile. "If you'll follow me, I'll see you to your fitting room. Can I get you or your friends anything?" she asked, giving the decimated truffle dish a pointed look. She reminded me of the counselors at the Lancashire School who would invite you into their offices, make you tea, sit you in one of their comfy leather chairs, and then ask if everything was okay at home, because something they called Big Life Changes could be stressful.

At least I knew this person's only ulterior motive was to stuff me into a bridesmaid's dress of pillow mint green. After motioning to Taryn to come with me, I smiled, set my teeth, and steeled myself for the inevitable. "Your boyfriend can wait here in the lobby," added the woman, smiling at Faris.

Ooooo. Was that ever the wrong thing to say. I stiffened, paused, and for a minute didn't even dare look at my future—my future what? What do you call a brother-in-law's brother? I started to turn around, aware that if I did, Faris would be wearing the most smug, insufferable . . . and there it was. A grin so horrible that it made me shudder. "I'll wait for you here, honeybuns," he called, waggling his eyebrows. Then he blew me a kiss. Peachy. Just peachy.

There's a point where you've got to draw the line. Why encourage him with a response? "This way," repeated the woman. I stepped off the Turkish carpet and onto the shiny wood floor.

"Hey, hold up." Faris ran up behind me and tugged at my wrist as I followed.

"What're you, some kind of changing room pervert, trying to get a peek at ladies' underwear? You can't come back here."

"I know, I know. I kind of want to tell you something." Like I wanted to listen to anything he had to say when I was still smarting from that boyfriend comment? "Something personal." I started to puff out my cheeks and blow air from them in an impatient kind of way, but something about the way he stood there, looking so out of place and lost, made me stop.

"Well?" I asked, annoyed after he did nothing but stare at me for a few seconds. I really wanted to reach

43

out and smooth down those eyebrows of his, but I kept my hands clutched behind my back.

"Okay," he finally said in a low voice. "It's only—I wanted to say thanks. You know. For what you did in . . . what you said in the taxi. Thanks." He shrugged. "That's all."

Oh. Here I'd prepared myself for something obnoxious and slimy and he was kind of behaving humbly. I hate it when I've worked up a nice grumpy outrage and someone rolls over like a puppy and shows his fuzzy little underbelly. Not that Faris was a puppy, but still. "Don't mention it," I said, trying not to sound caustic but hoping at the same time that he'd take me literally and never mention it to anyone.

He grinned after me. Maybe Faris wasn't so bad after all. Okay, so he'd tried to unhook my bra a year ago, but maybe we'd both grown since then.

"So that's pillow mint?" Taryn finally said after I'd been stuffed into Myra Chin's greatest-ever bridesmaid's dress. We were in the world's prettiest dressing room. Its wallpaper was red and gold and the space was filled with delicate antique-looking furniture. It was the size of my *bedroom,* and except for the multiple mirrors at one end it looked like some really rich person's boudoir. Myra Chin is supposed to be one of the top designers. I mean, movie stars wear her regular evening gowns when they accept their Oscars. Yet the only person who would have been caught dead wearing this fluffy, gauzy thing with its puffed-out sleeves would have been a demented clown from Ringling Brothers.

My reflection, poking out through the top of all the

toothpaste-green material, glared back at me from the mirror. Its face looked red and puffy. I turned away before I burst into tears at the sight. "What did I do to deserve all the bad luck in the world?" I wailed at Taryn. "I can't be seen in this God-awful piece of sh—"

One of the dressers poked her head in with a smile. "How's everything? Oh! Don't you look a sight! Aren't you something!" she crooned while she picked at some of the places where it didn't quite fit.

Somewhere in the back of my head I noticed that her words didn't exactly form a compliment. But I chopped off the rest of my curse and made my polite face. "I'm something, all right."

My words were enough to send her scurrying from the room in search of a tape measure. When I looked at Taryn, we both giggled at the close call. "It's not that bad," she suggested. "I mean, it's not like you have to wear it to gym."

I turned back around and tried to tame the crazy puffs of fabric around my legs. Maybe Myra Chin had invented the world's first anti-gravity dress. "Am I wearing this right?" I asked. I heard a rustle of fabric behind me. I thought it was the dresser and her tape measure pushing through the curtain, but when I turned, I saw nothing but white.

Molly, my sister, stood before me in her wedding dress.

I gasped. I don't know whether she was wearing a corset of some kind or whether it was the way the skirt of the dress spread out like a fairy queen's, but her waist looked thin enough for a man to put his hands around. She looked tall and regal; her hair had been

45

swept back and up and covered with a simple veil. The dress itself, though, was anything but simple—the white silk was covered with thousands of tiny, twinkling pearly beads. Molly had always been pretty, even during the thin, gawky, tinsel-mouthed years. In that moment, though, all grown up and shimmering, she was the most beautiful I'd ever seen her.

I wanted to cry. Part of me ached like crazy to be inside that dress myself, stunning as a dream and ready to get married to a man I loved more than anything. Another part of me was scared silly at the idea, and wanted to run far away and never, ever grow up. As much as Molly and I fight, I really felt like I was her sister, right then. Maybe pillow mint green was a small price to pay for this feeling. Maybe this wedding was going to make us friends at long last.

I gulped. This was like, one of those special moments I would remember for the rest of my life. I was seriously going to have an attack of the weepies right there! She held her arms apart, and I couldn't help but rush toward them for a loving, sisterly hug.

When I got within reach, she grabbed my cheeks and jaw with one hand and squeezed hard until I resembled one of those freaky breeds of fish with enormous flapping lips. Tears instantly sprang to my eyes. *"Listen, you little pissant!"* she snarled at me. *"If you keep trying to screw up this wedding, I am going to skin you alive with a potato peeler and dump your twitching carcass in a bathtub of brine so I can watch you SUFFER!"*

People always say Molly takes after my dad. I wonder why.

Taryn leapt up from her seat and jumped around

46

helplessly. I think she'd also expected something more along the lines of a Hallmark commercial than *The Texas Chainsaw Massacre*. "Eh *oh* oh eee!" I gurgled. It felt like she was ripping my face off.

"I'll let go of you when I've had my say," Molly growled, pulling my face forward until it was about six inches from her own. Oh, she had transformed into a fairy-tale princess all right, but beneath all the glitter and silk was the old wicked witch Molly I knew and loved. "I swear, I think you're doing this deliberately! Grow *up,* Beaner!"

She let go of my cheeks then. My hands instantly flew to massage blood back into them. It had been my sister who'd given me my nickname after I'd been born. Apparently *Hannah* had been too difficult for her to handle, and *Beaner* was as close as she could come. "I'm not doing anything!" I protested. As squozen as my face felt, her accusations hurt worse.

"My point exactly! You promised me you'd be *helpful* this month. You promised Dad and Jasmine you could be *trusted*. One stupid fitting! One stupid fitting is all I asked for and you couldn't even make *that!* Oh, God, I need to sit down."

"Here's a chair," Taryn said from behind her.

"I'm not *allowed* to sit down!" Molly shrieked, burying her face in her hands. " 'Don't sit down, you'll ruin the line of the dress, Molly.' 'Don't frown like that, you'll get wrinkles, Ms. O'Brian.' 'Don't talk that way, Molly. Brides don't say things like that.' And to top it all off, I've got a juvenile delinquent for a little sister who's hell-bent on making my every waking hour a living torture rack. Why am I doing this? Why?"

47

Despite the slam she'd given me—and I don't think that I'm hell-bent on making her life miserable by the way, it's just a by-product—she seemed to want some kind of sisterly response. "Because you love him?" I guessed.

"Oh, that's rich. You don't know anything about men! We could shack up for years if I loved him. Getting married is completely different." She batted at her dress with both hands so furiously that for a minute I was frightened those thousands of beads might pop off and fly around the room. "You don't know what it's like to stand here in one of these things and realize it costs more than your last two years of college put together, and know that once the ceremony's over, it's done. I'll be married. 'Til death do us part. Death! This is a designer prison made out of satin silk, that's what it is!"

"Hey," I said. "Calm down." Molly was seriously freaking me out. To be honest, I kind of expected her to fly off the handle at me. But all this other stuff—I didn't want to think about it. Way too scary. "You don't know what you're saying."

Molly's face started to redden, the way it always does when she's close to tears. "Oh, yes, I do. All Anas and I do is talk about stupid wedding arrangements. We don't talk about anything *real* anymore. There's nothing romantic about a wedding! I'm sick of it! I don't want to be Mrs. Anas Aloul. I don't want to get married! I want to move back home." She snuffled. Taryn dashed over to the table for a box of conveniently placed tissues. "Thank you. You're the only person who understands," she told Taryn.

"I understand!" I protested. I'd already been

48

alarmed enough with Molly wanting to move back home. Would she demand her old room back? I'd just gotten it the way I wanted!

"It's jitters," Taryn said expertly. She'd survived the weddings of her two older sisters, so I guess she'd know. "You'll feel different in a little bit."

"No, I won't." Molly looked longingly at the chair but didn't dare sit down. "This wedding thing sucks."

"Anas loves you," Taryn told her. "Plus he's a hunk. Hel-*lo*, have you looked at him lately? That dark skin? Those eyes? He's to die for."

Molly laughed a little and wiped the moisture away from her eyes. "Looks aren't everything," she said. "When I put on this dress a few minutes ago I looked at myself and wished that I could wake up and—and that this would all be a dream!"

"It's just jitters. Honest."

I felt awkward, fluttering on the outside of the conversation. Wasn't it supposed to be me saying all the reassuring things to my sister? Taryn, however, kept handing Molly new tissues and taking the old ones, all the while patting her on the back for comfort. Why wasn't that my first impulse? I only wanted to pretend nothing was happening. "What if it's not the jitters?" I asked. "What if she's got some serious doubts?"

Both Taryn and Molly glared at me. My sister looked stunned, as if I'd whacked her across the head with a concrete slab. Then she started to bawl. Taryn, on the other hand, squinted at me with annoyance. "Gee, thanks, Beaner," she grumped, riffling more tissues from the box.

"Ohhhhhhhh!" Molly wailed. "Anas deserves better

49

than an ugly cow like me! He shouldn't marry some-one who's having doubts!"

"Yes, he should!" I said, but that only made her howl more loudly. This was awful! I was getting every-thing wrong!

"Sssssssssh." Taryn went back into comfort mode. "You hush, now. Everyone has doubts before they get married."

"Really?" Molly asked.

Taryn nodded. "And no way are you an ugly cow You are beautiful, girl!"

"When I saw you walk in, I thought you'd never looked more beautiful," I added. For the first time that afternoon, I seemed to be helping. Taryn smiled at me in approval, and Molly even looked at me gratefully. "I mean, seriously gorgeous, Molly. I wish I looked half as good as you."

She sniffled. "Do you think Anas will think so?"

"Oh, yeah!" Taryn nodded at me, encouraging me to say something else. "He'll think you look great!" Molly laughed a little, adjusted her gown, and, I'm sorry to say, simpered a little. "Hey, Faris is out in the lobby. We could get him and see what he thinks about . . ."

Cue the music from *Psycho,* right before the scene that made me scared of showers for six months. "*Are you insane?!*" my sister screeched. "*You want to bring my future brother-in-law in here so he can go back to the Alouls and tell him how I looked like a total mess?! Three weeks before my wedding?!*" Her voice rose higher and higher as she ranted on. Across the entire island of Manhattan, canines were cowering down on the ground and trying to cover their ears as Molly hit

50

the ultrasonic frequencies. *"GET OUT! GET OUT! GET OUUUUUUT!"* she yelled at last, pointing at the door. Both Taryn and I fled before I even thought to remind her that she was in my dressing room.

It wasn't until the pillow mint dress was back in the hands of the boutique and the three of us were stuffed into the backseat of another cab that Taryn even dared speak to me again. "It's not only that you don't know how to talk to boys," she told me, nodding at my notebook. "I'm not sure you know how to talk to *people.*"

"That's hurtful!" I looked out the window. Early evening storm clouds hung over the skyscrapers, hiding their remotest stories from view. A lot of cars had turned on their headlights, giving the impression it was a lot later than it actually was.

"What happened?" Faris wanted to know.

"Nothing," the two of us snarled in unison. After the cab had pulled out into traffic and we'd made slow progress down the city streets back in the direction of the XT offices, I finally unclenched enough to ask Taryn, "I wasn't that bad, was I?" She rolled her eyes.

It started to pour rain. Thunder drowned out the sounds of traffic and car horns. Somehow it matched my mood. I hadn't meant to upset Molly. Maybe she was experiencing pre-wedding jitters, but how do you know what's jitters and what's real? How do you know if someone's *the one?* You see it in the movies all the time, men and women getting engaged when the real love of their life is someone else. Molly and Anas were the perfect couple—both so beautiful, him so accomplished, her so poised for success. But what if instead of being married to a hunky rising star in the investments field, she was supposed to be falling in love with some geek who repaired computers for a living? How was she supposed to *know*?

I was still moodily mulling it all over when the cab pulled up in front of XT's building to drop off Faris. "You wait here," I told Taryn. "No sense in you getting wet too. I'll get your bag and be right out."

"Thank you," Taryn said gratefully. See? I could talk to people. We ran like heck into the building while cold pellets of rain splattered against us.

Faris was quiet on the elevator ride up while I tried to shake the wetness from my clothing. "You and Taryn have a fight?" he finally asked.

"No." Explaining would involve too much effort. When I remembered the fuzzy underbelly Faris had shown me earlier in the afternoon, I couldn't help but soften up a little. "My sister's a freak, that's all."

"I think she's pretty cool. My folks really like her." Apparently Molly hadn't put any of the Alouls in a choke hold, yet. We rode in silence for a little while until we reached the studio floor. The bell rang. "You need me to go up with you?" he asked, his voice soft. "It gets dark upstairs."

"I'll be okay." He shrugged, stepped out, and started to lope away. "Faris?" I called after him, catching the elevator doors before they slid shut. I craned out my neck. "Thanks for everything today."

He grinned, almost like he was happy I'd spoken. "No problem, dude. Later."

The doors started to slide shut again. "Hey!" I called out at his back, catching them before they closed. "I am not a *dude!*"

My dad's office was in the boring part of the XT suites, a floor above the studios, where all the fun stuff happened. When I stepped out into the hallway, the place was freakin' empty. The hall lights had been turned off so that only a few recessed lamps spilled pools of light onto the carpet. Compared to the usual hustle and bustle, it was pretty eerie.

In my head I tried imagining where Taryn might have tucked her bag. I keyed in the punch-button combination on my dad's door and eased into the darkness, leaving the door open so that some of the light from the hallway filtered in. Sure enough, there it was, right under a chair, Calvin's signed CDs still sticking out from the top. I zipped it up, hauled the straps over my shoulder, and turned to go.

That's when I noticed the light in my dad's inner office.

Weird. He didn't usually stay past seven. "Video Request" was over by five-thirty in the afternoon, and although sometimes there was some cleanup afterward, seven was usually about the maximum he ever had to linger. "Dad?" I called out, working my way back through the gloom to his office. "Fonzi?"

Dad's desk lamp gave his office a browny-orange glow. When I stepped through the door, my eyes were first drawn to the array of glittering lights from the towering buildings all across the dark evening horizon. Maybe Dad had forgotten to turn off everything before he'd left.

"Who are you?"

I whirled around at the question. Huddled down on the sofa by my dad's door was a boy clutching one of the nubbly pillows. He had scared the living daylights out of me! My heart was still beating a mile a minute when I managed to choke out the words, "Who are you?"

"Who are you?" he repeated. He was maybe a couple of years older than me. Definitely seventeen at most. His face was long and oval, capped off by a few matted-down blond curls on his head. Even in the dim light I could see that his eyes were brown.

He looked incredibly familiar to me. Was he one of the interns? "Who are you?" I asked again. I could see this conversation wasn't getting us anywhere. "I'm Hannah O'Brian. This is my dad's office."

"Oh." The guy sat up, but still held the pillow as if for protection. Why did he look so recognizable? I knew I'd seen him before. I could almost come up with his name. "I'm Eug . . . onio."

"Eugonio?" I repeated.

The look of doubt on my face must've been pretty obvious. "Just Eugene," he said, flushing. His voice was soft. For the first time I noticed he was in trainers.

"What're you doing in my dad's office, Eugene?" I mean, he looked like a nice guy, and that whole soft-spoken thing made me want to cuddle him up and take him home like I would a really cute stuffed toy, but for all I knew he could've been a drug addict trying to rip off my dad for every valuable in his office. Which wasn't much, admittedly.

"They—they told me I could sit here for a while. I kind of got upset down in the studio, and Barry said I could cool off up here." I relaxed a little. That sounded like the kind of nice thing my dad might do, all right.

Studio guys could be a little rough on the new interns. Eugene looked up at me with interest. "So what's it like to be a talent producer's daughter? I bet you see all kinds of stars."

"Well. Yeah. A little." A very little. Like, nil. But Eugene didn't need to know I was playing cool. "You know. Now and again."

"So what kind of music do you like? Hip-hop? Electronica? Boy bands?"

"Boy bands?" Oh, the scorn! Maybe in the darkness I looked younger than fifteen, but I was not going to let anyone get away with thinking that I, Hannah O'Brian, sophisticated girl of sophisticated tastes, listened to that stuff. Even if I did, and secretly wanted to rub Kendrick's sexy little face all over my tummy. "Sheez, that crap? No one listens to boy bands. I'm kind of into, like, serious acoustic folk-rock with um, you know." I was in way over my head here. I searched for words that sounded good. "Political overtones."

"Cool." He nodded, a little smile on his lips.

"Hey, kid, I've got to—who are you?" While we had been talking, an older guy had walked into the outer office and flipped on the lights. He was shorter than I was—a characteristic you don't find in many fortysomething-year-old men—and balding, and wore a lot of gold chains around his neck. He stared at me like he wanted to beat me up. "Who's she? She bothering you? Get out of here, little girl. G'wan. Get out. Get out before I call security!"

I was not going to let some little roly-poly slimeball boss me around in my dad's office. "*You* get out!" I told him. "The security guards know who I am!"

"It's okay, Marty," Eugene said. "It's her dad's office. Right, Hannah?" I nodded and crossed my arms.

"Oh, you're Barry's girl?" said the Marty man. "Nice. Whatever. Now, g'wan. Scram."

"Marty!" Eugene seemed offended at my treatment, which made me like him a little more.

I was on Marty's insignificant list now, though. "Here, kid," he said, ignoring me and holding out something to Eugene. "I got one of the girls to press it for you so it's nice and neat. And here's your glasses." From his jacket pocket, Marty pulled out a pair of Oakley Quiksilvers with tortoise frames. Eugene sighed, took the shades, and put them on his nose. For some odd reason, that made him all the more familiar to me. "Now, listen up. They're waiting down in the studio." Marty started to say something about video monitors and I tuned him out as quickly as I tuned out my dad when he talked shop.

I looked at the just-pressed object that Eugene tossed from hand to hand as if he didn't want to put it on. It was a cap. An ordinary plain wool pullover skull cap, the in-style kind guys wore low over their brows so they looked like they'd just come straight out of the 'hood. You saw them in music videos all the time. But this was the bizarre part—sewn a couple of inches above the cap's hem were these weird clumps of . . . well, they looked like hair. Dark hair had been braided into little dreadlocks, so that if Eugene put the cap on it would look like . . .

Oh, no. Oh, *no.*

"Where are you going?" Eugene asked when I turned to escape. I couldn't look over my shoulder. I couldn't even say anything. I fled. "Hey, wait!" I heard Eugene stand up and follow me into the outer office.

"Gotta run!" I yelled and flew out the door. Oh, brilliant parting line, Hannah.

I did have to run, though. I had to run out of the building before I screamed. Why was I the world's biggest idiot? How could I be so *dumb?* On the trip down in the elevator, I mentally kicked myself a million times. Okay, so Eugene had resembled some random nerd when I first saw him, but those glasses—that *cap* with the Rasta braids hanging out. How could I have been so *stupid?*

Taryn gave me a peculiar look when I crawled back into the cab. "What happened to you?"

"Just *drive,*" I told the cabbie. He shrugged and pulled off into traffic while I looked back at the doors to the XT building. No one came out. Thank God.

"Hello?" Taryn asked. She helped remove her bag from my shoulder. "Did something happen?"

"You know Antonio?" I asked. "From S.W.A.K.?" Taryn nodded. I winced when I realized what I had to tell her. "His hair's fake. And his name is Eugene. *And because I am the biggest loser in the world I told him that no one listens to boy bands anymore.*"

Taryn stared at me in horror. I nodded emphatically as it all sank in. "Boy," she said, then whistled. "You really know how to charm a guy, don't you?"

CHAPTER ONE:

~~In today's world~~

~~There are as many approaches to finding a boy as there are girls who want to find a boy who wants to be~~

~~Ben Affleck + Hannah O'Brian~~
~~Come to dinner at Hannah and Ben's!~~
~~Mrs. Ben Affleck~~

"I still say," Carrie pointed out, yawning, "that Antonio doesn't have blond hair."

"She explained that." Taryn sounded pretty exasperated. She leaned forward over the middle seat of the van cab. The glossy book in her hands bore the title *Sealed with a S.W.A.K!* "Look at these pictures. Antonio's got on hats and big moofu sunglasses in every single one of them. He's the same way in all the S.W.A.K. videos."

Carrie seemed torn between keeping her eye on the

road for the cabbie and looking at the photographic evidence. Naturally she had called the van's backseat for herself, but Mandy and I had wedged ourselves in with her. The cab smelled like pee and air freshener. "You expect me to believe that all this time, Antonio has been some dweeby kid who sews dreadlocks into his hat so he can look more . . . more . . ."

"Happening?" Mandy supplied. She was curled up against the door, arms crossed, eyes closed. But then, we all were half asleep.

Taryn flipped more of the pages. There was S.W.A.K. joking around in identical track suits. S.W.A.K. covering a heart-shaped box of candy with pink plastic wrap. S.W.A.K. kneeling down on the floor with their shirts open and staring soulfully into the camera while . . . oh, my. I needed a cold cloth on my face, and on my neck. That's an understatement. I needed a cold beach towel to roll in, followed by a cold shower and maybe a trip to Norway for a long, icy dip in a fjord.

No. It didn't matter how S.W.A.K. might have made me feel when I was thirteen and only a kid. For Pete's sake, in less than a year I was going to be sixteen! Everyone was always telling me that's when life really started. You sure didn't see any of the older girls swooning over photos of Kendrick just because of the way his beautiful brown eyes looked out at you like a puppy dog who needed to be petted and rubbed and dipped into chocolate so it could be licked off all over its . . . oh, crud. Where were these awful childish feelings coming from, and wouldn't they *ever* turn themselves off?

We all lurched right then. The cab driver, a woman in her fifties with enormous freckles on her dark skin, had taken one too many sneak peeks at *Sealed with a S.W.A.K.!* and nearly rear-ended a city bus. Luckily at that hour of the morning there weren't many people on the road, so the three of us in the backseat very suddenly discovered who'd forgotten to wear deodorant. (Me.) "Sorry!" said the woman, looking over her shoulder. Taryn plucked the photograph book off Mandy's head. "It's only that that Kendrick boy is *so fine!*"

Okay. Maybe those feelings never go away. There was a depressing thought.

"You kids trying to get on 'A.M. USA'?" asked the cab's driver, her eyes once more on the road. "Awfully early, isn't it?"

For a minute I couldn't figure out how she knew what we were doing, but I suppose there weren't many other reasons a bunch of kids would catch a cab to Rockefeller Plaza at five in the morning. "We won't get a good place if we don't get there early," Mandy told her, once more trying to shut out the light of the streetlamps by shutting her eyes. "We want to be right up by the barricades."

"You girls must wanta see Marvin Carey do the weather and wish them hundred-year-old folks a happy birthday *real* bad, huh?" cracked the driver.

Taryn leaned forward, which at least gave me a little arm room for a moment. "S.W.A.K. is appearing."

The driver nodded. "Gotcha. You're gonna have some stiff competition for the good spots then, even at five-thirty in the morning."

I don't know whose idea it had been to get up so early to see the band perform. Mandy had been the one who saw the appearance announced on Friday's "A.M. USA." Taryn's the one who phoned the network to discover they'd be appearing and performing on the street. Pretty soon, Carrie was coordinating transportation and schedules. It's weird: At no point did we actually discuss going to see them that day, but somehow we all assumed we would.

What really burned was the way Carrie and Mandy seemed to be pushing us into going solely so they could prove I'd been mistaken in my dad's office. Oh, they believed I'd seen something, but they'd been a little condescending about it. *Maybe it was an intern after all, Beaner. Maybe it was a double for Antonio they hired for a decoy limousine, Beaner. Maybe you're a big baby, Beaner, with a baby's nickname who doesn't know any better.* They hadn't said the last part, of course, but it sure was implied. Even Taryn seemed to want to go primarily so she could prove I'd been right. She seemed afraid she'd chosen the wrong side of the argument by backing me. For a couple of years I'd been the cool one who was inches away from celebrity because of her dad's job. Now that I'd had a maybe brush with fame, I was suddenly back to being the infant of the group, the kid who didn't have a clue.

I'd never said it was definitely Antonio I'd met in the office. I'd said I *thought* it might be him. Antonio and Kendrick were supposed to be arriving in New York last Thursday afternoon. And they were going to the studios, right? And when my dad had been on the phone, hadn't he mentioned a Marty? I'm definitely not a baby. I can put two and two together.

My friends were patronizing me. Not a step of this trip was for my benefit, no matter what anyone said. It was that weird growing-up thing again. They were all pretending they were there for some kind of Sherlock Holmes sleuthing, a scientific analysis that would prove whether or not I was delusional. At the same time, though, they wanted to see Scotty, Wyatt, Antonio, and Kendrick, up close and personal, the way I did.

"Rockefeller Center," said the cab driver, pulling up to the curb. "Looks like you got here barely in time."

It wasn't exactly crowded, not that early, and the Center certainly wasn't bustling yet. Though its United Nations flags flapped in a light breeze, the only real noise came from the water of the fountains in the distance. Billows of steam from the manholes added to the dawn fog and made the scene look like one of those old movie musicals where someone skips down the sidewalk singing about love. When finally we were all out of the car and on the sidewalk, it certainly didn't feel romantic. All we did was shiver a little and make our way to the "A.M. USA" studios on the corner, where in big red letters the time was displayed in the ground floor windows. Like I needed to see clocks every ten feet? All I knew was that it was way, way, way earlier than I'd *ever* gotten up that summer.

The area had already been set up with big banks of speakers and a raised stage at one end of the street. Pairs of guys threw around heavy metal barricades like they were Lincoln Logs to make a long rectangular performance section. Looking at all the preparations made me feel jittery inside. Some of what I felt was plain old nervousness, but a lot of it was excitement. Were the others feeling it too? Looking at them, it was hard to tell. Carrie wore a bored expression, but even while her neck kept her head from turning, her eyes darted to take in every detail. Mandy seemed mostly to be yawning. Taryn was peering around, like she was trying to figure out the best place for us to stand. I put my hand on one of the barricade rails and tried to tell myself to calm down.

"This is *our* spot," I heard someone growl. I looked around, saw nothing, and then glanced down. Some ten-year-old blond girl stood next to me with her hands on her hips and her eyes screwed up into a death scowl. She wore a S.W.A.K. tour baseball cap on her head, sideways, like Wyatt in the "From Me 2 U" video, her braids hanging down her front. A S.W.A.K. T-shirt covered most of her body, and her hiking boots had undone laces like Scotty wore in "U Can Follow Me." She would have been the cutest thing ever if she hadn't looked like she wanted to beat me up in some dark alley and leave me for dead.

"I just got here!" I told her.

"This is my space and my mommy's space. Do I gotta whop you?" she demanded.

"Okay, okay!" I took my hand off the barricade and stepped away. Five-thirty in the morning and I'd already made an enemy for life. Sheesh.

"And don't come back!" Before I knew what had happened, the midget had kicked me right on the shin. I howled in outrage, then started after her.

"Don't pick on little kids, Beaner." Carrie yanked me

63

back, her tone annoyed. "Let's move down a little over here so we won't be looking at the band sideways."

Pick on kids! That little shrew had picked on me! "You better watch your back!" I growled over Carrie's shoulder. The midget stuck out her tongue. Geez Louise! She'd be pulling a switchblade on me next!

"Honest to God, Beaner, you're acting like a little baby. Stand still and don't get into trouble," Carrie ordered. Taryn and Mandy were already saving spots for us a few feet away, about halfway down the length of the rectangle. It was a little farther from the front than where the Bad Seed had been, but I could see this new position had a better view of the stage.

"What do we do now?" Mandy asked. She yawned again, but I could tell she was much more awake.

"We wait," said Taryn.

And that's what we did, after we elected Mandy to buy bagels and chocolate caramel lattes from a nearby coffee shop. The first half hour was the worst; everything around us was damp and kind of chilly and sleepy still. I could tell the others thought having to stand around was more excruciating than watching the famous Girl's Video in health class, but I kind of liked it. I drew a lot of energy from watching the city wake up.

Some people will tell you that the best time of day in New York City is at night, when the neon and lights blaze, giving the dark a fairy-tale kind of look. Other people say it's during the daytime, when all the tourist stuff is open and the city is bustling. But I've always thought the best part of the New York day is the morning, when everyone's rousing themselves and instead of diesel and car stink there's the smell of brewed coffee in the shops and pastries in the bakeries. It's when you see old men and women walking their dogs and enjoying the quiet, or joggers moving their lips in time with the music piped to their ears, or early businessmen and -women whistling on their way to the office. It's the time of day when nothing has gone wrong yet and anything seems possible.

Even when your shin is throbbing with pain because some lunatic escapee from a Swiss Miss box has whopped you good.

When we arrived, there had only been about a hundred people waiting for the barricades to go up; by six, the crowd had tripled. By six-thirty, the street was congested enough that we were having to give people behind us dirty looks when they tried to push their way forward. Taryn even had to speak pointedly to a basketball player–sized guy who tried shoving us aside. Things got really bad at six forty-five, when it seemed like every bus, taxi, and subway car in the city suddenly dropped passengers off at Rockefeller Plaza. I mean, that place was jammed. We couldn't even turn without getting intimate with the Korean tourists crushed up behind us. I mean, really chummy. I think I got to second base with one of them when I tried to stretch my shoulders.

"Oh, no!" Taryn yelled right before seven, when "A.M. USA" would go on-air. "I was supposed to call my mom and let her know I got here okay."

"You couldn't have picked a better time?" I complained when she thrust her bag into my stomach, trying to get her arm free. I ended up opening the bag's zipper and retrieving the mobile phone inside for her.

There wasn't much I could do about the noise, but Taryn at last managed to get some kind of message home by covering one ear, shoving the phone against the other, and shouting at the top of her lungs. Carrie borrowed the phone immediately afterward to do the same thing. "You want to make a call?" she yelled when she was done. She pressed the phone into my hand.

I shook my head. Making a call home was the last thing I wanted to do, I realized with a guilty feeling. I made a face and unzipped the outer pocket of Taryn's bag. She looked over her shoulder to watch me put the phone away, saw my face, and narrowed her eyes. "Something's up with you," she shouted.

"Nothing big," I told her. When she gave me the old distrustful eye, I crossed my heart. "Honest!" My grandmother was one of those old-school Catholics who thought of God as a big bloodshot eye in the sky itching to cast down lightning bolts and retribution on liars and sinners. Well, let me tell you—I would have been courting some major brimstone if I'd had to keep lying. Okay, so they were more like fibs. Little fibs. Tiny little white fibs that were more like mistruths than anything else. See, I hadn't exactly told either Jasmine or my dad that I was heading down to Rockefeller Center that morning. It's not that I was forbidden or anything. But I'd had the uneasy feeling that if I'd tried to ask, they would've told me no.

Fortunately I didn't have to endure Taryn's suspicions any longer, because right then the crowd nearest to the studio entrance started to yell and cheer.

The red numbers on the windows showed that it was two minutes to seven. I felt a flash of excitement as more of the crowd joined in with shouts and yells. Behind me, the Korean tourists were jumping up and down like crazy. Were the S.W.A.K. guys running out from the studio? Some guys were making their way from the studio doors—but when they made their way past the platoon of guards and burst out into the open area, it was pretty obvious that we were about to be subjected to some kind of warm-up band. Which entirely made sense. After all, "A.M. USA" was a two-hour show, and most of it was news and weather and interviews and all the boring stuff that would have put me right back to sleep, those mornings during the school year I wasn't already trudging my way uptown or sleeping in during the summer.

The warm-up band wasn't bad, but they weren't S.W.A.K. I don't think anyone in the crowd was really entertained by an anonymous quartet jumping up and down singing tunes from twenty years ago. I know I wasn't. Even weatherman Marvin Carey looked a little bored by the whole thing, and he's made a career out of being over-the-top happy. It was funny: at seven-o-nine and fifty-five seconds, when he was waiting for his first cue of the day, his face was totally blank. Then, right at seven-ten, when the cameraman pointed at him and the camera's light turned red to show he was on the air, Marvin suddenly became Mr. Perky. "And a hippity-hoppity good morning to you, America!" he shouted like some kind of bingo caller who'd been dipping into the happy hooch. Yeah, the guy was scarier in person than he was on television.

"We're here at the outdoor stage right outside the "A.M. USA" studios getting ready for a special appearance by Swack." Taryn and I looked at each other, ready to burst out laughing. "S.W.A.K., that is," he added, blinking rapidly and touching his earplug. Some producer must have been screaming into it for him to get the name right. "Quite a crowd we've got here today too! But first, your local weather." He grinned into the camera until the red light cut off and then went back to looking like someone's bald and grumpy grandpa.

And that's what we endured for another ninety minutes: occasional weather reports and long stretches of boredom. Our feet hurt from standing. We'd been shoved up against the barricades by the crowd behind us so many times that I thought I might have permanent grooves on my rib cage. We'd had our ears assaulted by an instrumental studio band playing everything from "Billie Jean" to "Venus" to "Smells Like Teen Spirit" and even a bad version of "From Me 2 U" like they were working a wedding. They'd launched into another vaguely familiar tune when I decided that this all had been an enormous mistake and that I should've stayed in bed all morning, because three hours on our feet guarding the same spot was torture, sheer torture. Taryn leaned over and yelled into my ear. "You should remember to tell Calvin about this!"

"About what?" I didn't have a clue what she meant.

"This!" she replied, gesturing. "This song!" When I looked even more blank, she looked at me like I was stupid or something. "It's 'Cigarettes in the Dark.' His second-most famous song?"

I guess that's the kind of thing you know when your mom is the country's biggest remaining Calvin Desburne fan. All of a sudden the cover band stopped playing, though, snuffing out the cigarettes before the chorus. The crowd got very quiet, like right before a play when the lights go down. I craned my neck around over the people crowding behind me. Even though the sky was cloudy and it wasn't too warm, everyone was sweating like crazy. The red digits on the studio windows declared it was 8:43. There were only a little more than fifteen minutes left in the show. They couldn't make us wait for *too* much longer, could they?

We didn't have to wait at all, in fact. The band started playing the opening intro of "Fly Tonight," the lines of security guards separated, and a quartet of guys came running out wearing tight white T-shirts, dark sunglasses, and tan overalls.

It was them. Ohmygod, ohmygod! It was S.W.A.K.!

I don't know which surprised me more, the ferocity with which the crowd started roaring at the sight of the band or the way I found myself joining in. It was amazing! On our side of the barricades we were some massive hungry animal that howled and hooted and jumped up and down and made a crazy noise that filled the city streets for blocks and blocks around. At first I was too stunned to take it all in. But there they were—grinning Scotty, with his curly hair and the dimple in his chin, the sharpest dancer and cute as could be. Wyatt, the soulful one, with his puppy-dog eyes peering over his shades, went through the steps like his heart was broken. Taryn kept on screaming Kendrick's name over and over again; his darker skin made his T-shirt look like some super-white fabric from a detergent ad. He kept throwing extra moves into their synchronized dance.

And then there was Antonio, with his white boy Rasta dreads hanging down all round his head, grabbing the mike and rapping out the song's introduction. It was funny how they all looked shorter and skinnier than in their videos. I hadn't expected that, but I didn't linger on the thought. I hadn't even noticed all the camera people until that moment, when a bunch of them converged to get good shots. We were on the air! The enormous speakers pumped out music at top volume, almost drowning out the crowd. Taryn grabbed my hand right then. When I looked at her and saw the excitement on her face, I knew it was a mirror image of my own. We jumped up and down and hollered like crazy little kids, excited as all-get-out.

I'm not sure what I expected from watching them. I guess I thought I'd savor it more—really relish it while it was happening. But on some level it was just too much for me. There was too much noise and too much motion, and there was the little girl in my head wanting to cry because she was so happy. At the same time, it was like all the rollercoaster rides I've taken. My body might have plummeted down to the bottom of that first hill, but my mind was firmly back at the station, worried about the trip up. By the time they caught up to each other, the ride would be nearly over. Why did everything have to happen so fast?

It's funny how sometimes, when something big is going on around me, my mind focuses in on the littlest things. Even though some of the biggest idols I ever had were only two dozen feet away from me—I mean, all my seventh-grade notebooks had their faces on them, years ago!—all I could look at were things like the way the clouds were speeding by overhead, and the way people beyond the plaza kept staring our way to see what was happening. When I saw a pair of sunglasses go bouncing out behind the barricade's braces to land on the ground a few feet away, I instantly stopped watching the guys dance and sing to focus on them. A little girl was leaning over the railing, pointing at them. Oh, heck. It was that evil munchkin again!

With all the music playing and everyone cheering behind me, though, it was kind of tough to keep up the ill will against her and her little steel-toed shoes. I mean, she was a S.W.A.K. fan, too, right? One of the security guards stood only a few feet away. Maybe if I could get his attention, he could pick up the kid's shades for her. I could earn a little good karma in the bargain, right? "Hey!" I yelled out, waving my arm at the guard's back. "Excuse me!"

When the big guy shifted slightly, I thought for a second he had heard me. Even at three feet away, though, my small voice was overwhelmed by the crowd. I signaled wildly with my arms one more time and pointed in the direction of the glasses. *"Hey!"* It was no use. That girl was going to have to wait until afterward to get back her shades, if they managed to survive without anyone stepping on them first. The boys were prancing around free-style now, while Scotty crooned his way through the vocal break. Every time they danced toward the barricades, the guards moved back without looking behind. Those glasses were goners for sure.

Someone saw me leaning over the barricade and gesturing, though. I was still so overwhelmed with the music and noise and even the smells of too many people standing too close together that at first I thought it was one of the crew who ran over to scoop up the little plastic frames, but when the boy straightened up, I saw the white T-shirt and recognized the overalls and the face.

Oh, no.

It was Antonio.

And he was heading straight for me.

CHAPTER ONE:

~~What is the key to finding a boy who can become not only a friend, but a love interest as well? It's simple! A boy isn't looking for a giggly girl. He wants a young woman—a mature young woman who not only knows how to keep her cool in any situation, but who can enjoy herself practically anywhere!~~

The security guard I'd been trying to flag down turned and looked at me like I was an enemy of the state. He barked something into a walkie-talkie that sat on his shoulder. I couldn't make out a single word Antonio said as he waved off the guard. Next thing I knew there he was, flipping up his head mic, holding out the sunglasses.

For a moment the only sound I heard was Carrie's operatic shriek right in my ear. I haven't *ever* heard cool, collected Carrie make a noise like that. It

73

shocked me. It was a little like finding myself in Oz and seeing Glinda the Good Witch suddenly rip off her fairy gown to dirty dance in tight spandex with the Scarecrow. Once my eyes stopped watering, I saw that Antonio had pulled down his own shades to look at me more closely. The second his brown eyes met mine, I knew he recognized me. "Hannah?" he shouted. He couldn't seem to believe I was there. Once again he held out the glasses. "Hi!"

Was it my imagination, or did he actually look pleased to see me?

"Antonio! I loooooooooove you!" Again with Carrie's eardrum-shattering yell! I wanted to muzzle her . . . with riveted iron.

"Those aren't mine!" It was the only thing I could think of to say. The shock of seeing Antonio—or Eugonio or Eugene or whatever his name was—was really too much for my poor overwhelmed brain. Even though I knew how totally stupid it sounded, all I could do was repeat myself. "Those aren't mine!" I said, accompanying it with an elaborate mime. "They're *hers*."

When I pointed to the Swiss Miss from Hell on the barricades a few feet away, he understood. "Don't go anywhere!" he shouted. "Okay?"

Where could I go? I merely nodded. Scotty's solo was almost over, and the four of them were supposed to go into harmony in mere seconds. Quick as a flash, Antonio handed the little girl her glasses and rejoined the group, flipping down his head microphone in time to start singing the final a cappella chorus with the others. Meanwhile, the pint-sized Queen of the

Damned shot me a look of hatred. If we had been in Oz, she would have been perfect as one of those nasty winged monkeys.

I was dimly aware that my friends were jumping up and down around me, screaming variations of *Ohmigod that was Antonio!* and *Antonio was talking to Beaner!* but I was still so stunned that I couldn't respond. Had I gone deaf? It was as if someone had pulled a blanket over my head, muffling every sound. I came back to reality as the band came back in with a final thudding chord to end the song, and the crowd burst into rapturous applause all around me. "She must be a friend of his," I heard someone say behind me. When I craned my neck to look, the woman caught my eye for a second, then deliberately looked away, embarrassed at being overheard. She had been talking about me!

I'm not used to that kind of attention. *Any* kind of attention, really. I'd always been the girl on the sidelines, and even being on the spotlight's edge made me want to pee my shorts. I would've slunk off to catch a train home if I could have, but there was no way in the world I could worm my way through that crowd. I was stuck.

Luckily the band went into another number. "I loooooove this one!" Mandy yelled, beating on the barricade so that it thrummed under my hand.

"*SWAAAAAAAAAAAK!*" screamed Carrie in a voice that could be heard all the way out to Long Island. I noticed that her hair had gotten loose from its tie and that she wasn't even bothering any more to swipe it behind her ears. Taryn jumped up and down and hugged me as best she could while the opening bars of "If I Could Give You (A Rose)" boomed out over the sound system. It was a sweeter number than the first; you could see the crowd visibly relax to the slower tempo.

7:55. It felt like they'd just begun, and here the show was almost over and I'd not enjoyed a single second. Wait. Yes, I had. At least after today, none of my friends would be able to deny I'd had a celebrity encounter in my dad's office. That alone made me grin. Okay, so there was still an entire mystery around why Antonio was calling himself Eugene, but I had my credibility back!

" 'If I could give you a rose'," they crooned in four-part harmony, " 'It wouldn't make up for the tears you cried—if I could give you a kiss, at least you'd know that I had to try—to win your love once more.' " It was almost enough to make me turn thirteen again, and stare at my school notebooks and wonder which one of the S.W.A.K. boys I wanted to lift my bridal veil at the end of the church aisle. Back then, I used to cheer and pray and make silent deals with God and the Virgin Mary to help their singles up the charts.

S.W.A.K. was out near the barricades now. Scotty, Wyatt, and Kendrick had all removed their sunglasses; all of them carried red roses in their hands that they rotated and tickled against their nostrils. " 'If I could give you a ring, it would be right from my heart'," they sang. Across the performance area I could see Scotty using his flower to caress the nose of a girl a little older than me. He kissed her lightly and handed her the rose. Kendrick worked the other side of the stage, gifting his rose to a little girl who didn't look old enough to know what was going on. And Antonio—

Antonio was heading right toward me. So that was what all my friends were screaming about! Even though I couldn't see his eyes for the dark lenses that covered them, I could tell that he was singing his little tenor heart out while he stalked toward me. I've never seen a car wreck, but suddenly I understood what people meant about how hard it is to tear your eyes away from one. Antonio's approach was a terrible, awful, horrifying sight, but I couldn't move. *" 'If I could make you my life, for every day of your life you'd know, it started with a rose,' "* he sang, and to my dazed ears it sounded like his voice only was coming out of the loudspeakers. He held out his hand. The flower trembled before me.

I think everyone in the immediate area went blue from holding their breath at the sight of us, frozen there in some kind of made-for-video tableau. That's when I noticed the camera, red light on, focused squarely on my face. I was being mortified right there in front of millions of people across the whole country. Peachy. My face felt as red as that rose. If my skin had been any hotter, I could have melted glass.

That's when Antonio moved closer, leaned forward, and turned his head to give me a kiss on the lips while he pressed the flower into my hands. It should have been the most romantic moment of my life. Instead, it felt like I was having my lips mooshed by someone with an over-fondness for expensive cologne and Listerine. On television. Coast to coast. With a bazillion S.W.A.K. fans all wondering why, out of all the actually pretty girls in the crowd, Antonio had chosen to yummy down on me.

Thankfully, there was no tongue. I don't know what I would have done if there'd been tongue. Screamed, probably, or bitten it off and had the death of a pop superstar by involuntary tonguectomy on my conscience for the rest of my life.

Then it was over. After distributing their roses, the guys drifted back to the stage and finished the rest of their song. The crowd burst into cheers and shouts and applause, begging for more. Then, waving their hands over their heads, S.W.A.K. ran through the lines of security guards once more and back into the studio.

It seemed as if their set was over before it began. When the loudspeakers went dead, my ears throbbed like they'd been assaulted. It took a minute for me to realize that as the crowd drifted away, I was hearing the normal Manhattan morning symphony of car horns and traffic and airplanes in the distance, and of people arguing and greeting each other, and of a crew striking the set and breaking down the linked barricades. It was done. In the "A.M. USA" studio windows, the clocks blinked 8:02.

"Oh, my God," I finally said. It felt like the first time I'd breathed since Antonio/Eugene had first spotted me. I thumped my chest to make sure my heart still beat. "Oh, my God!"

My friends babbled around me, but my brain still couldn't pick out exactly what they said. It sounded like they were telling me how lucky I was, and asking to see my rose. I couldn't let it go, though. Some part of me was afraid I might drift away if I did. Holding on to that rose's stem seemed to root me firmly to the ground. Letting go was the last thing I wanted to do, so I let them guide me along as we slowly walked in the direction of Forty-ninth Street.

"Hi?" Someone stepped in front of me. It felt like I woke from a deep sleep as I snapped to attention and took in the girl's pretty blond hair and S.W.A.K. World Tour T-shirt and the kid in her arms. . . . Aw, heck. It was Winged Monkey Girl and her keeper! "Hello? My girl has something to say to you."

The mother was awfully young—kind of like one of those characters from the health class Girl's Video about girls our age who got pregnant by mistake, only five years after shooting had wrapped. I blinked, confused. Were they going to thank me for getting someone to retrieve the hellsprite's sunglasses? How nice! I leaned down. "What is it, sweetie?" I asked.

The girl put her hands on her hips and looked back up at me and then uttered two magic words. "You *suck.*"

"Yeah, you *suck,*" said the mom, with a bray straight out of the wilds of Jersey. "That rose would have been *hers* if you weren't so damned selfish."

"I don't *think* so," I heard Mandy say. I was still too stunned to respond. "Antonio's my friend's personal *friend.*"

"Oh, *really,*" sneered the mother, putting the brat on the ground. "I didn't think Antonio would hang around with a *ho.*"

"A *ho?* Are you calling my friend a *ho?*" When Mandy gets into an argument, she really gets into an argument. She had her wrists glued to her hips, her eyebrows furrowed, and her lips wrenched into a scowl.

"Oh, man," sighed Carrie. Her voice sounded a little hoarse from all the yelling she'd done, and her hair . . . well, let's be frank. She looked like she'd been dragged backward through a hedge. "Taryn, you'd better get our little girl home," she said, nodding at me. "I'll extricate Mandy from 'The Jerry Springer Show' and we'll hook up later. Go!" she added, pushing at us. "Before Beaner gets into any more trouble."

I resented being called a little girl, but I felt as if I'd been on my feet for the last seventy-two hours and didn't have the strength to argue. It was obvious Carrie was trying to regain her status as the most mature of us—at my expense. I didn't resist when Taryn guided me away from the brawl in the direction of the nearest train station, or when she paid my fare and pushed me through the turnstile like I was some kind of helpless mental patient. I didn't object when she brushed my hair off my face and licked her finger to clear away a smudge on my forehead. And when she led me onto a train that smelled of cleaning fluid and urine. I didn't object when she sat me down onto the closest bench. I clutched my rose and trusted her to get me home.

I did, however, object when the old guy sitting next to me turned out to be my subway pal, Pervy O'Grabshimselfalot. "Hey, girly, hey, girly, hey, girly!" he cackled.

One word. Ew.

About a half hour later, Taryn steered me past my doorman and into the elevator. Even though it hadn't been overly hot outside, the air-conditioning brought me right back to life. "Oh, my God," I repeated. It had been the first thing I'd said during the entire trip. "Did all that really *happen?*"

"Larger than life," Taryn replied. "Wasn't it the best thing ever?"

"No," I said, quite honestly. "It was . . . *weird.*"

"Good weird or weird weird?"

"Kissing your brother weird," I said. The elevator chimed and the door opened onto my floor. I stepped out and slipped my key into the door opposite. "Keep your voice low," I warned her, "so we can sneak in. I didn't—"

I stopped in mid-sentence as the door swung open. My father stood behind it, his face looming over me as long and gloomy as one of those enormous Easter Island statues. "Hannah?" he finally said. "Maybe you've got something to tell your daddy about where you've been this morning?" When I didn't respond, he brandished the TiVo remote in his left hand and pointed it back at the television in the living room behind us. My face suddenly appeared on the giant screen, cross-eyed and dismayed, as an open-mouthed Antonio descended on my lips. In total, gruesome, excruciating slow motion.

My life as I knew it was totally over.

"I can't believe you didn't *tell* them you were going!" Taryn lectured in the privacy of my room a few minutes later. If my ears had throbbed before from the loud music, they really ached after hearing my dad ranting at the top of his lungs and grounding me until I was thirty-seven.

"He never would have let me! Dad thinks I'm a baby!" I couldn't even look at my best friend. I was miserable from seeing my misdemeanor on national television. That shot on "A.M. USA" made me look like I'd never been kissed before! The kids at the Lancashire School were going to be brutal come September! What if they all thought I was some kind of psychological nightmare, unable to kiss a boy? Worse, what if I *was?*

"You act like such a baby!" Taryn said. She was upset with me, I know, but mostly it was because she was worried I'd be stuck in my room for the rest of my life, like Rapunzel without the hair products. "Your father might have agreed if you'd only asked him!"

"He wouldn't. My life sucks. You can take the suckiest life in the world and square it and multiply by three hundred and it still wouldn't approach the magnitude of suckdom that is my wretched sucky existence."

At the same time Taryn sighed in exasperation, someone rapped at my door. I assumed it was my dad back for another tongue-lashing, but when I looked over my shoulder it was Jasmine. She was still dressed in one of the silk sheaths she wore to bed. It looked like some kind of Hollywood evening gown; an embroidered shawl hung around her shoulders. She carried a tray. I buried my head back into my pillow. "Go away," I commanded.

"I brought you girls *le petit déjeuner,*" I heard her say. I grumpily sat back up. Mood or no mood, I was still hungry. I saw her point to the gold pendant hanging around Taryn's neck. "I meant to tell you earlier that I was down with your chizzlin' bling bling, dear," she cooed. "It's the da bomb."

"Oh, thank you, Mrs. O'Br . . . Jasmine," Taryn corrected. I could tell she was blushing.

"Word!" Jasmine replied with a bright smile. "Now, I've brought you both orange-ginger French toast stuffed with a lightly herbed triple-cream Lombardy mascarpone, topped with thimbleberry preserves and mint leaves for garnish, accompanied by salmon roe on lightly buttered toast points. Everything a couple of homeys from the 'hood could ask for!"

"Nice," I muttered. "I'm grounded for life, I've had my lips assaulted on national TV, and now I get fish eggs for breakfast. Why don't you send down the lightning bolt, God, and end all this misery?"

Jasmine clucked, set the tray on my desk, then rested herself on the edge of my bed. "You know, when I'm feeling mopey and blue, I always do something good for someone else. It takes me out of myself for a little while and helps me appreciate . . ."

"That sounds awful," I interrupted.

"Now, Hannah," she said. When I wriggled my shoulder out from under her thin fingers, she sighed. "Although your father was in one of his moods—the sort where he reminds me I didn't give birth to you—I had a talk with him anyway." I knew Jasmine absolutely hated when my father made her feel separated from the rest of the family. "The good news is that he's not grounding you."

"What?" Even Taryn perked up at that one.

"You should have asked beforehand, but really, I

told him it's not that much earlier than when you leave for school."

Exactly right! I sat up then, feeling a little better, but still like a bone that had been left out for the dog to chew. "I know! I wish he'd realize that without jumping the gun! He treats me like I'm ten! I'm practically an adult!"

"Fo' shizzle, ma nizzle," she agreed in her cultured voice. When she saw me wince and cover my face with my hand, she looked puzzled. "What?"

"Jasmine, you're like listening to the Pope rap," I told her.

"What?"

"Never mind."

"I only meant that you're right. You are almost an adult. But the best way to make him understand that is to act like an adult would, which in this case means you should have told him your plans in advance." She smiled like she was making some kind of stepmother/stepdaughter connection, but I felt more like snarling. She was right—yes, she was right, right, right. I knew it at heart, and resented it with all my being. At the same time, though, there was no way my dad would have agreed to let me out the door that morning. My way had been the *only* way, and only through Jasmine's intervention was I going to be lucky enough to get away with my crime. "So tell me . . . was he a fly kisser?"

"Jasmine!" I had no intention of discussing kissing Antonio with my stepmother! Gross!

"She is *so* lucky," Taryn said. "Everyone around us was *so* jealous."

"Hannah doesn't like to talk about these things," Jasmine told her.

"She's still shy with boys. I don't know why. She's pretty."

"Word," said Jasmine. "Antonio would be lucky to have her."

"Antonio doesn't want me!" I had to say something to remind them I was actually in the room.

"Why not?" asked Taryn.

"Yes, why not, dear? It's not as if you have a big bodonkadonk butt."

Well, *that* was certainly nice to know. It only took one long, steady glare to send Jasmine from the room after that. Taryn hauled over the tray and we started in on the goop-covered, sticky French toast with our fingers. I wasn't much in the mood for conversation. It must have been contagious, because it wasn't until we were half finished that Taryn looked away from me and spoke. "You should have thanked her."

"Thanked who? Jasmine? For breakfast?"

"Not just that. For getting you ungrounded."

Oh. That.

Crud. But I could do it later, right? Even I wasn't convincing myself. A thank-you is never as good later on, especially when someone else has had to remind you to give it. It's all cold and meaningless by then. Maybe I was a selfish person.

I kept eating, stubbornly chewing bite after bite although I wanted to be left alone so I could have a good sulk under my covers. But would that really accomplish anything, or merely add to my misery? I wished for nothing more than to be anyone else right then—it was like Jasmine said. I wanted to take me out of myself. I couldn't do anything as corny as Jasmine suggested, though. I mean, good deeds for others? Come on! That went out with "Leave It to Beaver."

On my pillow rested the rose that Antonio had given me. Its stem was a little bent from where I'd clutched it so hard on the trip home, but the petals still curved away from the center like they'd recently burst into bloom. It was amazing how good looking at that flower made me feel.

That's when the idea occurred to me: an amazing plan that would not only make me feel better but would bring a little happiness to a couple of other people who needed it.

I mean, everyone likes flowers, right?

CHAPTER ONE:

Who: The opposite sex
What: Total domination by the female race
When: As soon as possible
Why: Because . . . (why???)

"But I'm allergic to roses," said Anas. My future brother-in-law ran a hand over his goatee and studied me like he wasn't quite sure who I was or why I was sitting across from him. I guess I did seem a little out of place in an enormous Wall Street office with a good view of the East River. Everything around me was glass and steel and reeked of money. I just smelled of Vanilla Coke.

With his dark skin, dark hair, and teeth as white as bleached towels at the YWCA, Anas always looked mighty fine. He had one of those faces that had been waxed and polished and exfoliated until the eyebrows and skin were perfect, and hair that had been tousled so thoroughly that you knew it took a hundred-dollar haircut, a gallon of guck, and a half hour in front of the mirror to get it just right. Usually I didn't like that kind of primping in a man, but on Anas it really didn't seem out of place. He was absolutely gorgeous in a *GQ* kind of way. Even with his expensive jacket off, his tie loosened, and the sleeves of his tailored shirt rolled up, he looked straight out of the pages of a fashion magazine ad. "The roses wouldn't be for you," I explained a second time. "They'd be for Molly. You'd send them to her apartment. I think it would be really romantic. Roses, a nice card, maybe a poem." Perhaps flattery was the right approach. "You're a romantic kind of guy, right?"

He still looked baffled. "But then I'd have to smell them," he said. "And I'm allergic."

"Why would you have to smell them?" The man simply was not making sense.

"When I went home?" Didn't he get the part where I said we'd send them to Molly's apartment? Finally he leaned back in his chair, interlaced his fingers, and explained in slow words, like I was a student who rode the special yellow bus, "Hannah, your sister and I are living together."

"Oh, my God, you two are *living in sin?!*" I yelped. I swear, I didn't mean to freak. Before his unexpected news I had been Cool Collected Girl, but after, I totally turned into the Church Lady. I mean honestly, you could have handed me a plastic rosary, tied my head in a white scarf for Mass, and called me Grandma O'Brian. I tried to save face. "Not that there's anything wrong with that, of course. Does, um, my dad know?"

"No." Anas didn't change expression. "Are you going to tell him?"

"No!" For a second I was totally cheesed I hadn't

heard about it from my sister. But then I realized that Anas was trusting me enough to share their secret. It felt good. It felt really good, in fact—young people against old people.

"I hope we can trust you." I beamed, though my sense of pride deflated with his next sentence. "Of course, Jasmine knows." Great. Jasmine was probably the one who *convinced* them to live together. She'd probably made them a little housewarming bouquet of bougainvillea and orange blossoms tied together with ribbons hand made by Tibetan monks. Oh, of *course* Jasmine knew. Still, keeping a secret like that from my dad was better than nothing.

"Are you like, using the same bed and everything?" Instantly I knew that was the wrong thing to ask. I mean, who could sleep at night knowing there was a hot 'n' hunky Jordanian heating up the sheets in another bedroom? Certainly not Molly. "Sorry."

Happily, he seemed more amused than annoyed. "Hannah, is there a particular reason you've come down to give me lessons in flower-giving? Are you working on commission for FTD?"

I let out what I hoped was a carefree laugh. "No, nothing to worry about. I just thought, you know, flowers. So nice! But honestly, Anas, do you think that you and she are—wait a minute. How *long* have you been living together?"

"Seven months," he said. "Do you have a problem with us? Maybe I shouldn't have said anything."

"No, I'm cool. I think it's great," I lied. I didn't want another repeat possession from Grandma O'Brian. Seven months! That would have been like right after the holidays. Had Molly bought my Christmas presents knowing she'd be living with her boyfriend only a month later? Had she been, like, *thinking* about it while she bought them? She'd given me a sweater of sin! I'd worn that thing all winter! "Really great. Really, really—" When he looked at his watch in a surreptitious kind of way, I knew I was getting off track with all the reallys. I had to get back to the heart of the matter. "Anas, have you and Molly been . . . you know. Close, lately?"

His dark eyes, so very much like his brother's, stared at me while he considered the question. "Sexually close?" he finally said. "This morning; why? And last night, and yesterday before dinner—"

Whoa, whoa, whoa! That alone was *way* more information than I ever wanted. "I didn't mean *sexually!*" I interrupted quickly, before he could get into the kind of territory where my ears would be so polluted that I'd have to slice them off with a flaming letter opener and cauterize the eardrums with red-hot Q-Tips. "I mean, not only sexually. Everything."

"She has seemed a little distant lately," he admitted. "Last night I asked her about it."

"You did?" That sounded encouraging. "What did she say?"

"Well, it was in the middle of our lovemaking, and I looked down and saw that she wasn't, you know, totally involved in what we were doing. I wasn't sure if it was me, or whether it was because we were in the kitchen. So I—"

Ew! Ew! Ew! I'd made myself grilled cheese sandwiches in my sister's kitchen! I rose to my feet before he said anything else I didn't want to hear. I'd done the job I intended to do by asking him about flowers, but a bunch of roses weren't going to fix the problems of two people already living together. I was in way over my head. "You know," I said, "I'm sure you've got work to do and I've got to be—anywhere other than here. Okay. Nice talking, Anas."

He looked absolutely baffled. "But—"

"Buh-bye!" I turned to go, but before I eased myself out of his office, a thought occurred to me. "Does Faris know about . . . you know?"

"Me living with Molly? He ought to. He helped me move in." He laughed.

Ooooo, it figured there was a vast conspiracy against me. In my imagination I could see Molly and Anas and Faris and Jasmine sitting around a dinner of, I don't know, some weird imported herring fondue that Jasmine had made from a recipe handed down by her Viking great-great-grandmother, making plans without me. "Don't tell Hannah," I imagined them whispering. "She's only a baby. She won't understand."

What kind of person did they think I was? I thought about it as I walked toward my dad's office, keeping enough of my brain alert to the traffic crossings. Did they think I was Hannah the Tattletale, who'd go running to Dad with the news? Did they think I was Hannah the Delicate, who couldn't stand the notion of my sister and future brother-in-law doing the deed before marriage?

Or did they simply not think about it at all? Did they assume I was Beaner the Baby, and that my opinion or trust didn't even count? That was the scariest thought of all.

I found Faris on my dad's floor, running around with boxes of CDs in his arms. "Hey!" he said, his arms hanging low from the weight. "What's going on?"

"I know you're working and everything," I said, "but I kind of wanted to talk to you a few minutes. Alone?"

His expression went weird right then. For a second he looked as if he didn't want to speak to me at all, and then he looked like he was happy about it, and then he frowned again. "Um, let me check on something." I waited against the wall while he disappeared with his load. People passed me in the hall, but I was such a semi-familiar sight on the XT offices floor that the most attention I got were little absentminded smiles. When Faris returned, Hamilton was at his side. Faris murmured something up in the direction of the other intern's ear, looked at me, and then murmured again. Hamilton nodded.

"Hey," said Hamilton, nodding at me. Lordy, he was gorgeous. Where's a lifeguard when it's painfully obvious someone's been double-dipping in the good gene pool?

"Ham and I have switched some assignments," Faris explained. "It's cool, right, bro?" he asked.

"Yeah. Hey, Hannah?" asked Hamilton. "Are you going to see your friend Taryn anytime soon?"

"Probably." Hmmm. Maybe they were really hitting it off after all. "What's up?"

"I was wondering if you could maybe give her a note for me?" With his second and third fingers he plucked a folded square of XT stationery from his T-shirt pocket. "I didn't get her phone number when we had lunch."

That was definitely Taryn; her motto was *give them*

a little less than enough and leave them wanting more. "No problem," I said, taking the note and putting it in my sweater pocket—well, Jasmine's cotton sweater, really, since I'd snitched it from her closet that morning. I get cold easily, and she'd never notice one light sweater missing. Would it be an invasion of privacy to read it? Oh, yeah! Did I want to anyway? Utterly. "I promise I'll get it to her."

"So come on," said Faris. "We've got a few." He dragged me in the direction of the elevator. When we crowded ourselves in, a bunch of serious-looking executives from the upper floors sniffed at us like we carried cooties.

I didn't want to talk to Faris surrounded by suits, and when we were outside the building and on the street, it was way too noisy. "Where are we going?" I yelled at him as we tried to make the light by running as fast as we could in front of honking yellow cabs and a furniture delivery truck.

"You'll like it," he told me. "It's a fun place."

"You're not going to get into trouble for switching jobs with Hamilton, are you?" I shouted.

He looked over his shoulder at me. "You care?"

What did that mean? Did he think I was totally heartless? "Yeah, I care. I don't want you fired or anything."

The fun place turned out to be a little shop on a side street three blocks away, in the basement of an old storefront. Bolts of fabric were stacked in its windows. I was about to complain that in no way did I consider fabric shopping fun when Faris pushed open the door and I found myself standing in a wonderland that made Alice's seem like the 'burbs of Teaneck, New Jersey.

It was some sort of costume shop, or maybe a vintage clothing store—whatever it was, there was something to look at everywhere I turned my head. Old dressmaker's dummies stood right inside the entrance, wearing long beaded dresses from the Roaring Twenties, each head decked with darling little hats with feathers and pearls. Snazzy zoot suits lay on a worktable nearby, their lapels marked with chalk. A cloth measuring tape lay atop them. On blank-faced heads all along the tops of the dark wooden cabinets sat more headgear: English bobbies' helmets, golfer's caps, top hats, a knight's metal visor, women's hats from every century, and even a football helmet. A long rack carried all kinds of men's pants, each marked with a yellow tag, and on another were women's dresses of so many styles and sizes it was impossible to take them all in. I saw boxes of scarves and gloves stacked on every flat surface, and one entire wall of shelves holding shoes. Black shoes, white high-heeled shoes, old-fashioned boots, and even a pair of ruby slippers were set side by side in their cramped quarters.

It was like the biggest dress-up attic I'd ever seen. A little old man beetled over to us, peering through his wire spectacles at the sheet Faris pulled from his pocket. While they consulted, I decided now would be the ideal time to satisfy my curiosity about Hamilton's note. I wedged myself between a rack of uniforms from armies past and present on the left and a bunch of bustles on the right and retrieved the fold of paper from my pocket.

Hey hot stuff—
It's true, I've had my eye on you ever since
you first came down to the XT. Let's do
something Saturday night? See you then.
—You know who

Not exactly the kind of communiqué that would surpass Romeo and Juliet as the hottest couple in romance, but it had a certain kind of attractive nonchalance. Although I'd figured it was my prerogative to snoop, I'd immediately felt a little embarrassed when I peeked. My nosiness really wasn't very grown up, was it? Why did I do stuff like that?

"Hey." I nearly started out of my skin when Faris's voice sounded immediately behind me. I quickly folded up the note and put it into the pocket of Jasmine's sweater, then tried to seem casual when I turned around. "What're you doing?"

"Um, nothing," I lied. I saw him looking at my hands plunged into the sweater pockets. Now would be a good time to distract him. "This is a crazy place, huh?"

He grinned. "Hold still." Faris turned and reached over a circular rack of print shirts that could have appeared on any episode of "Laugh-In" and produced a white feather boa. He draped it over my shoulders and then pulled off another one for himself. Magenta. Very tasteful. "You look like a hooker." He laughed.

"Yeah, well, you're a transvestite hooker. So there."

He seemed to take it like a joke, which was a good thing. The Napoleon Bonaparte hat he pulled over his head made him look completely demented. "So you wanted some quiet time? Alone?"

"Oh." I felt a little uncomfortable even talking about it, once he reminded me. "It's about Anas and Molly." When he nodded and started rummaging around in a box, I cleared my throat. "You know they're—you know. Living together?" I took the beaded headdress he gave me and put it on my head. I didn't know what kind of person would wear such a thing. Maybe a high-class Pharoah's wife in a biblical pageant, or some demented flapper.

"Yeah." After a second, the implications sunk in. "Oh, wait. You didn't."

I shook my head. The beads rattled so much that I took the headdress off. "Not that it's a big deal or anything. I'm cool with it. Because I'm a cool kind of girl. Who's cool with that kind of thing if everyone else is cool with it." I was painfully aware that every time I repeated *cool*, I sounded more and more uncool. "So it's . . ."

There was no way in the world I could allow that word to come out of my mouth again. I snapped my jaw shut. Faris waited a second, then grinned. "Cool, maybe?" I flushed. "Hey, Hannah, it's okay. I guess I might be a little on the freaked side if I were just finding out. I mean, when Anas was moving in, I thought, whoa, this is kind of big-time stuff, but then I thought, hey, why not? If no one's getting hurt, and if the parents don't find out—"

"Wait a minute," I interrupted. "Your mom and dad don't know either? Would they be upset?"

"You kidding?" Faris's eyes bugged out. "If they

found out he was shacked up, forget forty years of Americanization! They'd be shipping him to my cousin Jasim in Amman to be married off to some Jordanian girl in a yashmak. Heck yeah, they'd be upset! They're all about the marriage vow. It's a promise. Promises are important to our family."

"And to you too?" I asked him.

He nodded. "I mean, you give your word to someone, you should keep it. No excuses. You just keep your promises."

Faris seemed so certain about the issue that it made me stop and think. Over on the other side of the shop, the little old man laid a couple of coats covered with plastic wrap on a table. They were obviously part of the order Faris was picking up for the XT. He then disappeared into one of the back rooms again, muttering to himself. "It's weird," I said, watching him go. "You get this mental image of your family, you know, and for years at a time it doesn't change. So in my head when I picture Molly and me, she's like, fifteen and in braces, and I'm a kid, all of nine. I used to follow her around everywhere, then. It was crazy." I didn't know why I was telling Faris my thoughts, but he had leaned his elbow atop one of the racks and was resting his head on his hand, listening and nodding. It felt comfortable, I guess. "Everything she did, I wanted to do. If she took ballet lessons, I wanted ballet lessons. It drove her mad. But you know, when she went off to college it was like she closed some kind of door in my face. All of our faces. I mean, we didn't know her friends anymore, didn't know what she was doing every minute of the day."

"She was just being her own person."

"Yeah, I know, and that's the kind of thing you're supposed to be happy about." He nodded at me. When his bicorn slipped forward over his eyes, we both laughed. I reached up and adjusted it for him. "I was, you know, a crazy kid. At heart I wanted the best for her. Only today, when I found out she had this thing going on with Anas—which is cool, really it is—it felt like when she'd slammed the door in my face, she'd meant it for good. I mean, it took a few years, but she totally forgot I was on the other side, waiting. Now I know we're like, two totally different people, and it's really for forever."

Where had all that come from? I guess I was letting loose with everything I'd been bottling inside for a while. Had I said too much? I looked up at Faris, a little nervous at his reaction. I didn't know whether I'd be angry or relieved if he responded to my speech with a joke. My confession had left me feeling, well, naked.

He gazed steadily at me for a moment. When finally he spoke, his eyes were sleepy-looking and he wore a smile. "You're not that different from Molly."

"Are you kidding?" Surprising, how bitter my laugh sounded even to my own ears. "You have no idea what it's like to be the ugly duckling in the family where your older sibling is a gorgeous swan."

"You think?" Even I, who had somehow overlooked her sister's living arrangements for months and months, couldn't miss the twitch that convulsed his face. Instantly I felt awful. If there was anyone else who would understand that particular sentiment, it would be Faris. Gawky Faris, with his big head and bristly eyebrows and enormous hands, who probably had grown up the second banana to his flawless older brother. I instantly wished I'd kept my big fat mouth shut. At last he looked away. I thought he was trying to figure out a way to tell me to mind my own business—and I would've deserved it. Instead, he turned back without a trace of humor in his eyes and said, his voice low, "Even the ugly duckling got a makeover."

A half dozen different thoughts went through my head. Was he talking about himself? If he meant me, was he implying I *was* ugly? Why in the world was I at all concerned whether or not he cared?

More importantly, why was I moving closer to him, and why was he moving closer to me? I reached out to straighten his magenta boa. It was a nervous gesture, nothing more. When I felt the heat of his body through his T-shirt, it surprised me. None of my friends had skin so searing. My hand stopped, resting on his chest.

In the quiet of that musty old shop, standing only inches apart, we could hear each other draw every breath. I hoped he couldn't read my thoughts. I was frightened to guess them, myself. I rested the palm of my hand on the light muscle of Faris's chest, across where his heart lay. Odd, how I could feel it thumping beneath skin and flesh and bone, one steady beat at a time, while my own pounded away like the combined percussion sections of all the marching bands in the Macy's Thanksgiving Day Parade.

Somewhere deep inside my brain, I wondered if I was doing the wrong thing. Only in some freak show version of the universe could I be attracted to Faris. My older sister's maybe-husband's younger brother. That was practically a recipe for monster mutant albino babies with giant heads, wasn't it?

At the same time, though, I didn't move away, and neither did he, not even when the gap between our mouths started to close. The warning voice in my head grew louder. If I kissed him now . . .

Up close, Faris looked more like his brother and less like the kid I'd always thought him. If I kissed him now, hard . . . what?

"Um." He started to straighten up, then paused and looked at me as if trying to make up his mind. Finally he stood back up again. "Man."

I tried to laugh it off. That had been a close call. "Sorry," I said, mortified that the lion's share of the blame had been mine.

"It's not that I don't want—I really don't want you to think—I mean, when you said you wanted a couple of minutes alone—" A variety of emotions seemed to cross his face. It was hard to believe that only a moment before we'd been that close to . . . you know. "That's probably not what you meant. Alone, I mean. Like, *alone* alone. I don't want you to think I assumed you meant—"

"No, no, I get it." I honestly did, despite my confusion. "And when I said a couple of minutes alone, I didn't mean—you know. I honestly did want to talk to you, but not, uh . . ." He stared at me intently while I spoke. "It's about flowers."

"Flowers?"

To my ears it sounded like we were babbling. I tried to get things back on track. "This is kind of heavy stuff. Can you keep quiet about it from your family?"

His heavy eyebrows quirked toward his nose and he crossed his arms. "Yeah, sure, okay." I explained to him about Molly in the fitting room, and the doubts she'd had about marriage. "Aw, that's just nerves," Faris finally said. "All brides get nerves."

Where was the engraved stone handed down from Mt. Sinai that declared *all brides get nerves?* Was it in a shrine somewhere? Why had everyone visited and read it but me? "I had this idea," I said. "I thought maybe if we sent some flowers in Anas's name . . ."

"We?"

". . . that Molly might, you know. Soften up a little."

"Why do you want to meddle in their affairs?"

I hesitated. I was still feeling a little strange from that near-kiss encounter of only a few minutes before, but refurbishing Molly's shabby romance was something I really wanted to do. Everyone was always pointing out what a terrible sister I was, right? Now I'd seen a way to make it up a little, and Faris could be my best ally. "It's not meddling. Not really. It's—it's a random act of kindness. Totally anonymous."

Faris still looked unconvinced. For a moment I regretted confiding in him at all. "I don't think it's fair that Molly gets all the attention," Faris finally said. "I mean, guys like flowers too."

"Send flowers to Anas? From Molly?"

I must have sounded incredulous, because Faris nodded. "Why not?" He sounded stubborn. "Or else I'll tell."

"Tell what?" I asked, only half as outraged as I tried to sound.

"I'll tell your dad about them living together."

I'm always amazed how stupid the male sex can be. I mean, one minute they're acting like grown-up Romeos and then the next they're back to being little boys in the sandbox. "You do that. I'll tell your mom and dad the same thing, only I'll tell them you knew all along." That seemed to get him. His jaw flapped open, then shut again. I only barely managed to refrain from adding, "Nyah!"

"Okay, okay, truce." He waved his hand around like it held an imaginary white flag on a stick. "If you want me to help, I think spreading the love should go both ways, that's all. Molly's the one who's close to breaking a pretty serious promise to spend her life with him. I don't like promise breakers."

I wanted to defend Molly. It's the O'Brian family pride. I didn't have an answer for him, though. I didn't have a clue whether it was Molly or Anas or nerves or gamma rays from space. "How do you know it's not your brother's fault?"

"I don't know how any man who loves a woman could not want to make her totally happy." The words came out with considerable force, surprising me. Then he shrugged. "I want Anas happy too."

It grated a little that he was making conditions. At this point I could either choose to go off on my own or I could accept it and work with him. A few moments ago after our whatever-it-was, I would instantly have said no. But thankfully, that momentary blip on the radar seemed more and more unreal with every passing second. "Okay. Deal."

"Cool." Faris grinned. When he loomed closer, I worried he was going to kiss me for real this time. He only held out his hand. "Shake?"

We sealed the deal. "And about that—you know . . ." I started to say, embarrassed.

"Yeah, let's forget it!" His zeal to disregard our moment almost offended me. I mean, was the prospect of a smooch with me *that* disgusting? Since I was the one urging him not to mention it again, though, the idea of asking seemed a little ungrateful. I turned to lead us out of the maze of clothing racks. "I probably couldn't have compared to Antoooooonio, anyway," he said in a mocking voice.

"What?" I whirled around. "You saw that?"

"*Everyone* saw that, doof." He laughed. "It's cool. Don't be looking like I poked you with a hot fork." When he saw how upset I must have seemed, his voice got more soothing. "Aw, don't be like that. I didn't mean anything. It's all about the publicity with those kinds, right?"

"Right," I replied, feeling a little shaky. Then, sharply, "I hope you didn't think you could plant your lips on me because I've been kissed on national television."

"Plant my lips on you!" He laughed, pushing past me to where the little man was counting up receipts behind a table. "Yours were the ones doing the chasing, you know."

"Oh, they so were not."

" 'Oh, Faris!' " he said in a goony voice. " 'I'm so *hungry* for your kisses. I want you to *take* me. Take me like Antonio would!' "

103

I rolled my eyes. We were back in the kiddie pool again. Considering my recent dip into adult swim in the deep end, it seemed a lot more comfortable place to paddle around.

CHAPTER ONE:

What's that tingle you feel when a boy's near? It's love. What's that sparkle in your eye when you step out into the street? It's love! What's that feeling in your stomach when you see the boy of your dreams?

"Nausea?" Calvin suggested. When I jerked my head up from my new start, he had his arms crossed and the kind of bitter expression you might see on someone's face after they'd taken a mouthful of super sour candies. Minus the drool. "Because that stuff's makin' Calvin sick."

"Aw, man!" My notebook went right back in my lap. "I have a whole page more like that! No good?" I could tell he was searching for a tactful answer. I decided to save him the effort. "Okay, okay, I'll toss it. But that was the best start I had yet!"

"If that's the best, it's a good thing you didn't show Calvin the others," he rumbled.

"My deadline's in less than three weeks!" I wanted to throw the darned notebook against the wall. "I've got to get something down on paper. Five thousand words! Nothing I've written so far has turned out right."

"Child, it's not good because it's not *real*. And it's not real because you're thinking you can get any old thing down on paper and get away with it." I turned away to hide my disappointment. It had taken me all last evening to write that page and a quarter. He was kind, but every word still hurt. "When you try to sit down and cogitate and elucidate and assimilate something that's not in your heart, it's gonna be hard work. If it feels like you're working against the grain, you're not keeping it *real*. You've gotta start over. If you write about something that's true and real, it's going to pour out of you like a waterfall and it's going to be like the sweetest music you've ever heard."

To me, the lecture sounded like every pep talk ever given to me by an adult. What did Calvin know about anything, anyway? The thought occurred to me that if he was such an expert on life, he'd actually have one, instead of sitting in my dad's office all day. Unlike every grown-up who talked to me, though, I didn't feel it was my place to lecture other people about their shortcomings. I sat there and nodded and nodded, and nodded some more while he talked and waited for him to finish.

"Sssssssssheeeee," he finally swore. "You ain't listening to a thing Calvin has to say. You do it your own way then, and when you find out Calvin was right, he's only gonna tell you the three magic words."

"I love you?" The guy was baffling me.

"I told you so." He stopped and thought about that one a minute. "Told. You. So. Three words."

"Uh-huh." I tried not to smirk, but my laugh came out through my nose.

"Child, you can go on in and harass your daddy instead of making Calvin Desburne's life miserable."

"Hello? Like, he's not here?" Fonzi's desk was deserted and my dad's office door was shut tight. I'd checked out my dad's electronic planner pretty thoroughly the night before and knew I had only a narrow window of opportunity to corner Calvin while they were in a production meeting. I was keeping an eye on the outside door, just in case. "I came mostly to see you."

He was instantly suspicious. "Why?"

"You're the world's expert on love, right?" It was probably too late to sweet-talk him, after the attitude I'd thrown a moment before. I decided to be frank. "I have a friend who needs a little help in that area."

"Oh, a *friend*, hmmm?" Calvin rubbed his beard with the back of his hand. "And what kind of help does your *friend* need?"

I barged right on. "What I'm really looking for is the perfect note to send with a nice bouquet of flowers. Not an apology or anything, and not anything too mushy." I couldn't imagine Anas writing a sonnet to Molly, or anything flowery. "Something that says, hey, you're pretty cool and I'm thinking of you."

Calvin had been regarding me steadily during my request. A smile briefly crossed his lips. "What would *you* say?"

I bit my lip. "Hey, you're pretty cool and I'm thinking of you?" When he registered exasperation, I rocked back and forth in my chair. "I don't know! That's why I'm asking you! You could have any woman you want with your smooth talk!"

"Child, you're thinking Calvin is a lot bolder than he actually is. Here's a little secret, between you and him: He's pretty shy when it comes to approaching a lady for the first time. But after that, the loooove instinct takes over." When I stared at him in utter disbelief, he half-rose from his chair and then sat back down again to face me better. "Sad but true! Calvin's had his eye on a certain foxy lady for a while now, and he's not been able to make that first move yet. Every time he sees her, though . . ." His gaze shifted somewhere far off, and his hands began to trace curves in the air. "He can tell she's *magic*. Every day when he sees that special lady, she moves past him like Queen of the Nile. Every red-blooded man wants to be her servant of loooove. When their eyes meet, his heart starts to beat, for he longs for his sweet, his oh-*so*-petite—"

"You're going to start to sing, aren't you?" I interrupted. "I can always tell. Who *is* this foxy lady?"

He broke out of his daydream and looked at me warily. "None of your business." Hmmm. When in the world did Calvin have time to see a woman, every day? All he did was sit here in my dad's office. Wait—was it possible that the lady was someone at the XT? Crazy! Maybe Calvin came in every day not only to sit here and visit with my dad and read his books, but so he could catch glimpses of his Queen of the Nile walking up and down the hallway outside! I perked up.

The thought of Calvin being all stalkeriffic suddenly made him more tragic and interesting. "Put this down," he ordered, gesturing at the little card I'd selected for the flowers. "You are—"

A thought struck me. "Can you write it?" I pleaded. "I'm not sure I want my handwriting recognized."

Calvin looked at me thoughtfully, then took the pen and card and began to write. *You are what gives this city its romance,* it read. *I love you, baby.*

"Awwww!" I said. "That's great!"

"Of course it is. Calvin wrote it," he said, obviously proud of himself. He tucked the card in the envelope and flipped it over. With the pen he added a few words on the outside of the envelope. *To Faris. From Hannah.*

"*What?!*" I shrieked. He seemed surprised at my reaction. Then again, I suppose screaming at the top of my lungs, grabbing the card and divesting it of its wrapping, and shredding the envelope into a hundred pieces would startle anyone. "Why'd you write that?"

"Don't be going postal on Calvin," he said. "When you told me it was for a friend, Calvin thought—"

I groaned. "Oh, I'm *so* not that transparent! I didn't mean *me!*" I looked down at the card in my hand. At least it was salvageable. I supposed it didn't need an envelope. "And why Faris?" That was the question that bugged me most. Had Faris told people about that weirdness in the costume shop? I'd kill him if he had. That possibility nagged at me, but I really couldn't see him confiding anything to Calvin. The has-been singer was mere background to most people.

"He's been out in the hall sneaking looks at you. Don't go looking, now!"

Too late. I'd already whipped my head around and caught Faris peeping in through the blinds. He held an oddly shaped package that I could tell contained the flowers I'd sent him to buy. I motioned at him to come in. "There is nothing going on between us," I hissed at Calvin as I stood up to open the door. "I don't know how you could think that."

Calvin shrugged. Faris stuck his head around the door. "Is the coast clear?" he asked.

"Get in here." I closed the door behind him and shot Calvin a wide-eyed look that was intended to say *I don't know why in the world you think that Faris and I have anything going when it's perfectly obvious that he's like, so totally freaky that it's not funny,* although it probably looked more like *Hey, watch me make a face like I just inhaled laundry powder and I'm about to sneeze out my brains through my nostrils.* The singer looked at me like I was crazy, rolled his eyes, and went back to his book.

Faris crept into the office cuddling the wrapped flowers in the crook of his elbow. "I didn't want your dad to see them," he whispered.

"Dad's not here. You can drop the cloak-and-dagger act," I said, giving Calvin a significant glance to indicate my distaste for the idea of all things romantic that involved Faris. I got the impression from the way he refused to lift his eyes from the pages of *Gone with the Wind* that Calvin was ignoring me as hard as he could. "Put them on Fonzi's desk, I guess. I'll put the card in."

Faris watched while I tried to undo the staples at the top of the package until I punctured the end of my thumb so that it drew a spot of blood. Finally he plucked a staple remover half-hidden among the files and directories off the desk. He didn't hand it to me right away, though. Instead he held it above my outstretched hand. "Hey, I know you're going to take this over to your sister's bookstore after this, but I was kind of wondering if you wanted to like, you know, ditch the haute cuisine this evening and get a pizza or a burger or something." From the far corner of the room Calvin let out a loud and meaningful cough. Before I could respond, Faris added quickly, "So, you know, we can talk more about what we're going to do for . . ." He lowered his voice. "Molly and Anas."

His request made me impatient. I mean, withholding the staple remover? So childish. I had to remind myself that Faris and I were in this scheme together. For better or for worse. Ooooo, bad choice of words—too close to marriage vows. After the wedding and after school started back up, the only times I'd have to see him would be at joint family functions. Until then, I had to maintain cordial relations. "I think that'd be fine," I said. "Maybe I could swing back by at about six-thirty or so, post mission accomplished?"

"Yeah? You'll come right back?"

"Sure. I promise to." A wide grin flared up on his face, then disappeared, squelched. I thought my words might put him at ease; I knew how much promises meant to him. "I mean, yeah. Cool." He dropped the staple remover into my palm. "We can talk about stuff."

When the last of the pesky little staples had finally tinkled onto the pile on Fonzi's desk, I peeled open the paper. The fragrance of roses, stronger and sweeter than even perfume, almost overpowered the room. I love roses. Their bouquet seemed to fill the office with the scent of some faraway garden back in courtly times, where knights jousted for the honor of speaking to fair ladies. I know it's silly, but that's what roses always make me think of, and I'd never smelled so many of them at once before. It was like getting a heady whiff of pure romance.

A little plastic holder sat in the middle of the bunch, a generic blank card sitting in it. I plucked it out and substituted the one Calvin had written for me, mourning for a moment the envelope I'd had to tear up. Still, this was going to be one irresistible package. I could imagine Molly getting it and running home to Anas's arms, where she'd declare her love for him and they'd—well, do the things that couples do when they make up. Only I hoped they wouldn't do it anywhere out of the ordinary again. I mean, ew. I have to visit that apartment sometimes.

I was chunking in the last of the new staples when the office's outer door swung open with a burst of noise. "I can't believe this mess," I heard my dad saying. I hurried to get the flowers fastened again, nearly having a heart attack when the package almost flipped off Fonzi's desk. I moved it more to the center and turned around and tried to look innocent. Faris moved beside me and crossed his arms.

"If you'd calm down," Fonzi argued back.

"Calm down! Oy! How can I calm down when

I'm—Oh. *There* she is." He was talking about me. Dad halted in the middle of the room, hands on his hips. Behind him, Fonzi carried an armful of papers, glossy folders, big floppy books, and plastic wallets filled with slides, topped off with a laptop. She was clearly struggling to keep it all balanced, but when my dad slammed to a stop, she careened into him and things began to spill. Calvin dropped his book onto the chair I'd recently vacated and raced to her rescue. She gave him a grateful look right as they managed to save the computer from slamming to the floor. My dad kept talking while they attempted to salvage his things. "There's the little girl I've spent a lifetime raising and protecting, and who's gotten everything her heart desires ever since she was two and wanted a Baby Curly-Pop doll. She had to have a Baby Curly-Pop doll," he told Calvin, ignoring the fact that his friend was on his hands and knees picking up slides. "Just had to have it. Then it was Barbies and braces, and soon she'll be wanting college and cars and God knows what else. Hail Mary, full of grace, the Lord is with thee, because he's certainly not with me and my out-of-control daughter."

I was so confused and guilty, though I didn't know what in particular I was supposed to be guilty of, that all I could say was, "It was Molly who had braces."

"Listen to how she talks back to me! Would you listen!" He held out his hands in appeal as Fonzi and Calvin scurried to the desk to deposit their burdens. "And you! What are you doing here?" he added to Faris. "This is family business. Get back to work!"

I'd forgotten that Faris still stood beside me, but I

was suddenly grateful for his presence. Maybe he could be like, the airbag that cushioned me from the impending crash. "He's going to be family."

Creezus, you could actually hear Dad's teeth grinding! "I'd better get going," Faris said, pushing himself up from the desk. "Dinner tonight, right?" I nodded and gave him a little mortified wave as he snuck from the office.

Dad watched him go. "Dinner? With a boy, no less. No dinners at home for Little Miss-does-what-she-wants."

"You never eat at home during the week!" I shouted, still not understanding what all this was about. "What is your deal?"

Calvin slunk by on his way back to his seat. From behind me, I heard Fonzi disappear into my dad's office. It was obvious they were pretending not to hear the nuclear explosions going off in front of them. My dad decided to try a different tack. "Beaner . . ." he started off gently.

"Hannah." I hated that nickname!

"Beaner, you're a little girl. You're too young to date. Especially one of these . . . pop star types."

"I'm not dating anyone!" I said. Was this about Faris? Because if it was, everyone was getting way out of line. Math might be my weakest subject, but I knew that one weak moment on my part did not equal a sudden boyfriend. "I don't know anyone I want to date! It's a hamburger, Dad. Chill or something!" Suddenly the rest of his sentence sunk in. "Pop star types?"

"Beaner, for your father's mental health, put your

hand on your heart and swear to Jesus and Mary and to all the saints that you haven't made promises to this boy that you can't keep. I swear to God, if you have—"

In school we once read about Lizzie Borden, this woman who one day got fed up with her parents and hacked them to death with an ax and somehow managed to get away with it. Right then, I felt a lot of empathy for old Lizzie. *"What boy?!"*

I must have been loud enough to shock my father into silence. He looked over his shoulder at Calvin, and then at Fonzi as she emerged from his office, but they both averted their eyes and went about their business. "Antonio?" he said. "Antonio Diaz? From your favorite band?" My brain suddenly went sludgy. What in the world was he talking about? "The one you kissed in front of God and forty million people?"

"I know who he is," I said, closing my eyes at the memory. "But what's he got to do with me?"

"You mean to tell me you *didn't* ask him to ask you to take you on a date?"

I had to sort through that one for a few seconds. "No! As if. Please."

My dad crossed his arms and sneered. I recognized the look of triumph. He used it whenever he thought he'd won an argument. "Then why is his manager strongly urging me to set it up? I mean, he didn't actually *say* that S.W.A.K. might not appear on 'XTreme Video Request' Monday afternoon if I don't expedite it, but the implication was there. Wasn't the implication there, Fonzi? I believe the implication was, indeed, there."

I didn't actually reel back at the news, but it certainly felt like I'd been pummeled with a cannonball. "*Dio mio,* Barry, I told you maybe the kid likes Hannah, simple as that. It can happen," Fonzi snapped behind me.

"She's a baby!"

"She's fifteen!" This was one argument I decided to let Fonzi handle. "She's growing up!"

"No, she's not! Not if I can help it!" I gaped at Dad's words. I'd known he'd been trying to hold me back. Fonzi grumbled. Even Calvin looked up and shook his head. "Well, she's not old enough! Boys are animals! She doesn't know!" I was about to speak when he started in again. "Oh, fine, now you're going to say I'm overprotective. Well, maybe I am! The girl doesn't have a mother!" Once again, he started arguing with himself. "I know, I know, she has Jasmine. But she's a little baby!"

"Dad—"

"Oh, hell." He sagged. "Give your daddy a hug, honey." I fell into his outstretched arms and let him squeeze me and kiss the top of my head. I still didn't know what the heck was going on, but I knew it had something to do with Antonio. Which flabbergasted me. I mean, what the heck? I couldn't wrap my brain around it. "You'll be a good girl, won't you? Do you like this boy?"

"Dad, I don't even *know* this boy!" I yelled into his armpit. He wrenched my head free and held it between his hands as he looked to see if I was telling the truth. "Honest!"

Dad let out a long, sad sigh. "Let's give them a call, then. Don't agree to anything you don't want to," he warned. "And you have to be home by ten. Nine-thirty." He pulled his electronic organizer out of his breast pocket. "And if he tries anything . . ."

I closed my eyes, absolutely mortified. "Dad!"

"I'm just saying is all. Here we go." While studying the organizer, he reached for Fonzi's phone. "I swear to God, I don't know why I'm doing this. I know, I know, she's growing up, she's not a little girl any more. . . ." He handed me the phone. "Go on, take it. And be polite."

"Who am I talking to?"

"Antonio! Here!" He pushed the handset to my ear. I could hear it ringing on the other end.

I looked at him in a panic. Why was this all going way over my head? Was I on "Candid Camera" or something? "What—?" I began to ask, but right as the word came out of my mouth, someone picked up on the other end.

"Yo, dawg, wha's kickin'?" The voice sounded so vivid and crystal-clear that I could practically name the flavor of gum in the speaker's mouth. " 'Sup? Who dat?"

"Um." I was finding it hard to breathe. "May I speak to Antonio?"

"Marci?" said the voice. "Yo, Marci, my lady of the stars! You usually be callin' on Saturdays. What's up with my astrology, dawg? You callin' to tell me that my Mars is in retrograde or Uranus is in my crib or somethin' like that?"

"Um," I repeated. It seemed to be the only word I remembered. "I'm not Marci. My name is Hannah O'Brian and—"

117

"Hannah?" Antonio seemed utterly surprised to hear my name. I could have sworn I heard something fall onto the floor. "Hey! How are you?"

I was intensely aware of my father's eyes on me as I talked. I tried to ease the distance between us by stretching the phone cord so I could sit at the end of the chairs, next to Calvin. Fonzi lifted the phone and set it on the edge of the desk. "Was that you, just now?" I asked.

"Yeah." He sounded embarrassed. "I gotta, you know, keep it real and stuff." To me it had sounded anything but real, but I let it pass. It was beginning to sink in that Antonio was talking to me. To *me!* "You there?" he asked. I had spent so much time absorbing the situation that he probably thought I'd gone out for pizza and forgotten to hang up.

"Oh, yeah. So what's up?" I said, adjusting my shorts and trying to pretend I was cool and calm and collected, when really I was red and flustered and probably shooting steam from my ears.

"Not much. What's up with you?"

"Not a lot." With any other guy I would've thought it a boring start to a conversation, but my brain flashed everything he said in neon: *HE wants to know what's UP with YOU!*

"So . . ." he finally said, after clearing his throat for a few seconds. "I was kind of thinking maybe you wanted to, you know, hit the town tonight, grab a bite, hang out. That kind of thing. Nothing major."

Oh, my God! Oh, my God! He was totally asking me out! A boy was asking me out! Not any boy. I was scoring a date with one of the most popular boys in the history of mankind! Girls everywhere kept Antonio's photo inside their lockers and on their notebooks and mirrors and hanging on their walls. But he wanted to take out *me!* I was going to be the date of S.W.A.K.'s hottest boy! Okay, so he wasn't the hottest, or the second-hottest, but he was mine for the night! I'd be leaning against Antonio and wearing big dark glasses and holding up my hand and murmuring "No photos, please," whenever we stepped outdoors. I was so going to be the Yoko Ono of that band when Antonio started his solo career. Girls everywhere were going to hate me for breaking up S.W.A.K., but I wouldn't care. I would be notorious. My friends were absolutely going to pee their pants!

This was the sort of thing running through my brain as I said, like it meant nothing to me, "Sure. Okay."

I heard a catch in his throat. "Great." He sounded relieved. Did he really think I'd say no? Did anyone say no to someone like that? How crazy! "I'll get my people to call your people and I'll pick you up at seven. Sound good? You got my cell number, right?"

Sound good? It sounded like the best offer I'd had in fifteen years. When I hung up the phone, I was glowing. Glowing! Everyone I knew was going to be totally looking at me in a different light now. I would be a celebrity date! The thought was one half-cup excitement and two cups total freak-out, put into a blender, pureed on high, and served over ice.

"Well?" My people—a.k.a. Dad—practically had veins popping from his forehead. It was enough to bring me back down to earth. "What? What fresh hell are you going to inflict on me now?"

"We're only going to get something to eat to-night," I told him, trembling. When he started to show the signs of a brain aneurysm, I calmed him down. "I'll be home by nine-thirty! I won't let him 'try anything'! Dad, I'm not ten!"

"That's great, child," I heard behind me. "Calvin thinks that you're really growing up. Isn't she, Fonzi?"

I looked over to the assistant's desk to see her reaction and got the shock of my life. Fonzi had the goofi-est look on her face I'd ever seen—the kind of expression women get with their newborn babies, right after they've been pushing them out for fifteen hours and they're finally snuggled down in their arms. Except in Fonzi's arms wasn't a fat little bald baby. It was two dozen roses, long-stemmed, with a card lying atop them that I could tell she was reading over and over.

Dad took one look at the flowers, shook his head, and stomped into his office. "Women," he muttered.

"Hey!" I protested, rising out of my seat.

I was surprised when Calvin yanked me backward and pulled me into the hallway. The office door slammed behind us. "Now, now," he said in a whis-per. "Let's not be hasty or nothing."

"But she opened Molly's roses!" I protested, oblivi-ous to the people walking around us. "I've got to tell her they're not for her!"

Calvin looked pained. "Now, why you gonna go and do something like that? She'll be all crushed, after they went and made her feel good."

"Hello!" Another shush from Calvin made me lower my voice. "That's sixty dollars from my savings account!"

120

"I'll give you seventy-five if you just—" Calvin suddenly seemed speechless. "Just let her be, for now."

I looked through the blinds at Fonzi, who seemed absorbed in her own little world. "And she's not going to be disappointed when she realizes they're from nobody? Who would send Fonzi flowers?" Calvin watched the assistant too, a strange expression on his face. "She's going to think they're from you, you know, if she recognizes that handwriting."

"She might," Calvin admitted. Right then, Fonzi looked up from the roses and smiled through the blinds at the two of us. It was the strangest expression I'd ever seen on her usually professional face: private and even a little saucy. Calvin grinned so wide I could practically count all his teeth, even the gold one toward the back. "But that's a chance Calvin's willing to take."

CHAPTER ONE:

~~THE BOY BAND'S GIRLFRIEND~~ (ick! I'm
not dating all four!)
~~GIRLFRIEND OF A SINGULAR BOY BAND~~
~~MEMBER~~
SHE'S TOP OF THE POPS!
All eyes are on her when she's in view, her
hand on the arm of one of Billboard's
highest-ranking music celebrities. As the
flashbulbs of the ~~papparotzo papappaparazzi~~
paparazzi explode like a lot of (exploding
things) [fix this later!], she steps from her
limousine and says

"Aiiiiiieeeeeeeee! Ohmygodohmygodohmygod!" I had
to hold the receiver away from my head so that Taryn's
death screech didn't shatter my skull into a thousand
pieces. Not a bad general idea to keep the receiver as
far from my face as possible, considering it looked like
front-runner for the title of Most Germ-Infected Pay

Phone Mouthpiece in Greater Metropolitan New York City. "Where are you? What are you doing? Is it fantastic? Did he kiss you? Has he like, totally yummed down on you? Tell me everything! Wait! Don't! Why are you calling me in the middle of your date? That's so totally not right. Why are you calling me? I'm *sooooo* glad you did! Tell me everything! Oh, my God, I wish Mandy and Carrie were here. I'm going to call them the second you hang up. Well? *Say something!*"

Two girls and a guy shoved past me in the dark hallway, laughing and giving me sideways glances as they passed. None of the three were more than a couple of years older than me; the girls had dark hair and white makeup and looked like utter Goths. One of the girls' elbows knocked the receiver from my hand so that it battered against a wall covered with graffiti and what I hoped was nothing ickier than gum. Not that my two-fingered grip on it was all that tight, mind you. They all disappeared into the women's room together, arms around each other's necks. I listened to their laughter echo after the door closed, then scrabbled for the phone once more. "Hello?" I heard Taryn asking. "Hello?"

"Sorry, dropped the phone," I whispered, but to be heard over the noise from the front room I had to repeat myself.

"Listen . . . are you okay?" she asked. "He didn't like, use his celebrity status to, you know, seduce you and then like, drop you off under a bridge near the docks? Beaner, that's straight out of a really bad movie! What happened?"

"No." I felt caught between laughing and crying.

But what had happened? It was way too difficult to explain on the phone, in that dark hallway, in that awful place where I was afraid to touch anything—or anyone. Only two and a half hours before, I had been sitting in my dad's bedroom at Jasmine's dressing table, letting her apply more makeup to my face than all the members of KISS combined, while she gave me hints about ladylike behavior on my date. "And Hannah," she said, stippling some kind of highlight to the middle of my eyelid, "if your young man should proffer any illicit substances—keep your eyes closed, please—whether it be 'smack' or 'pot' or a questionable vintage of wine—" She made little quotation marks with her forefingers as she talked.

"I'm a minor," I reminded her. My everyday conversations with Jasmine always gave me the sensation that they couldn't be happening, but added to the excitement I was feeling about seeing Antonio, this tête-à-tête seemed particularly surreal. "I'm not allowed to drink wine. No matter what the vintage."

"That's scandalous," she murmured. "Why, my *maman* and *papa* shared the table wine with me from the time I was six." Well, that might account for some things. "But if something like that happens, what did I tell you to say?"

The doorman's buzzer interrupted the quiet. Jasmine swooped across the room to answer it. "I can handle myself," I assured her.

"What did I tell you to say? Say it with me."

I groaned, but her face clenched. Trust me, when Jasmine's face clenches, I have to hear the comprehensive list of all the muscles strained on my behalf for days after. I sighed deeply and repeated the words with her, though I would rather have a trick tooth hiding a capsule of cyanide than ever have to say them aloud to anyone else: *"Yo, boo, you be straight trippin'."*

"That's right," she told me, pushing the button. "Yes, Roger?"

The doorman's voice sounded positively agitated through the little speaker. "There's a little guy down here asking for Miss Hannah?"

My heart began turning cartwheels. That little guy was mine, all mine! "She'll be right down," said Jasmine. She came back across the room. "Well! Don't you look lovely. I'm so proud of you." She fluffed out my hair. "I'm sure your father will be. I know that if your—she—" Her voice trailed off, but I already knew what she'd been about to say. If my mother were still alive, she'd be proud of me too. I liked that thought, and I almost liked Jasmine for thinking it.

Dad didn't look that proud when I stepped out in the hallway, though. With his crossed arms and sour face, he looked like he was trying out for a part in *Pissed: The Musical!* "Nine-thirty," he growled.

"Ten," said Jasmine in a gentle voice.

"And don't expect me to come bail you out when you land in the pokey."

"Call if you have trouble."

"Woman, why do you contradict me!"

Jasmine shot my dad a dirty look. "Don't ever say those things to your daughter. Even in jest."

"My daughter," said Dad. "*My* daughter." I could tell Jasmine was upset at being excluded. She turned white as printer paper. If looks could have killed, my dad would have been skewered and skinned and roasting over a hibachi.

"I'll be back later," I said, taking the chance to slip out the door before the bickering began. When Dad and Jasmine have their once-yearly fights, it's hurt feelings for miles and miles until they make up again. I felt badly that this one was brewing over me, but I was too giddy and excited and scared and freaked and late to stay and listen to the fireworks. With the door closed, I heard their voices rise in anger.

But I tried to forget it all on the elevator trip down. I had a more pressing concern. What kind of person was I going to be for the evening? Any one who's ever been a teenager knows what I mean. You have to play different parts all the time. We're one person for teachers, one person around our parents, and a totally different person when the door's shut and we're among friends. My natural instinct was to be Overwhelmed and Out of Her Element Girl, but no one likes to hang around those types. No one likes Giggly Goof either, or her cousin, Miss Wallflower, so those were out. And I definitely wasn't taking a trip to 'Ho-ville.

So I decided that I'd be Cool Confident Young Woman, someone who wouldn't be fazed by anything thrown her way. I'd be nonchalant, like Carrie. I'd hold my head up high and smile mysteriously, like Jasmine. I'd even be flirty, like Taryn. I had a lot riding on this date—my first ever and very possibly my last if it went badly—so I was determined not to be the kind of girl a guy wished he'd never hooked up with in the first place.

Beyond our building's front doors I could see a long black car parked at the curb. A *limo!* Holy cats! My heart began to beat faster. This is what being grown up was all about: limousines, nights out on the town, and glamorous intrigue. "Hi, Roger," I said to the doorman.

He had his arms crossed and his face drawn into a smirk. "Evening, Miss Hannah," he said, rising up from his seat.

Our building's doormen still wore old-fashioned uniforms. Roger tipped his hat slightly as I glided past him, while I wished I had a fake fur (impractical) or a long black scarf (unlikely) to throw back over my shoulder in a show of luxurious abandon. Instead I had to make do with fiddling with the amethyst pendant under my cute black blouse while pretending that gleaming black cars picked me up every night. "Many thanks for notifying me of my conveyance, Roger," I said graciously.

"Um, Miss Hannah?" he called after me as I swanned my way toward the limo. Then he pointed at it and shook his head. "The limo's for Thirteen D. You're over there." He pointed at another car a good ten feet up the street.

At the Hooptymobile.

You know that terrible jarring, screeching sound old-fashioned records used to make when you'd suddenly yank their needles across their grooves? Yeah, that's the sound I heard in my head when I realized that the car waiting for me was an ancient souped-up Cadillac convertible the color of a magenta Crayola, painted with red and orange flames on the side. Behind its tinted glass windows thumped a sound system bass line that had to be registering on the Richter scale. In case I didn't get the message of what kind of wheels I'd be riding in for the evening, all I had to do was look at the license plate: PMPDADY.

I had to ride in *that?* It was awful! I wanted to turn around and race back up to my safe little bedroom and hide, but I knew my dad would say *I told you so* and turn me into his own personal Rapunzel, only without so much hair. Despite the sinking feeling overwhelming me, some part of me still playing the part of Cool Confident Young Woman made my legs slink over to the pimpmobile. Where was Antonio? Why wasn't he standing outside the car waiting for me?

Scarcely had I reached the curb when all the doors of the car popped open and a hundred people got out, like one of those clown cars at the circus. Well, there weren't a hundred, but there were a lot of them, and I surely didn't recognize a one. They all stared at me—guys in oversized street clothes with crossed arms and girls with their hands on the hips of their tight pants—not saying a word.

There was something horribly wrong about the entire situation. It felt like one of those TV shows where a girl's walking down an alley late at night wearing skimpy clothes, and you roll your eyes because you know her pretty little neck is going to be the midnight buffet for a vampire gang before the next commercial. There was no way I was going to be the girl with the Swiss cheese neck. I turned and was about to run back up to our apartment, even if it meant having to tell my dad that he was right, when the thundering hip-hop music dampened and I heard a voice from the open back door of the car. "Hannah?"

When I looked over my shoulder, I saw a wool hat, white-boy dreads, long sideburns, and an absolutely ginormous pair of red-tinted sunglasses leaning out. Relief washed over me at the sight of Antonio's toothy smile, but his friendly expression disappeared, as if he suddenly remembered I wasn't the only one around. He crossed his arms and jerked his head. "C'mon, babe." He stroked the seat and slid back into the depths of the car. "Yo, c'mon y'all!" he encouraged, when I didn't move. "Genuine leather interior!"

Yeah, that's how you weaken a girl. Who can resist sweet-talk like that? Still, putting my butt on genuine leather with Antonio sounded a lot better than taking my butt back upstairs. Without saying anything, I clutched my bag to my chest and slid into the car. "Yeah, that's right, babe," he said. "Everything's cool. You like my ride? It's my Seventy-five Cadillac El Dorado. Yeah, El Dorado, you can't beat an El Dorado, right, bro?" he asked one of the people crowding back into the car. "Y'all, this is Hannah. Hannah, these be my peeps."

His peeps? They were yellow Easter chicken marshmallows? "What kind of name is *Hannah?*" said one of the girls in the front seat, turning around to stare at me like I was the new kid in school and she was the self-appointed bully.

Before I could talk, Antonio spoke up. "Yo, yo, yo, don't be talkin' smack about my lady. She's got *soul.* Anyway, I call her Lady B, for O'Brian. Ain't that right, Lady B?"

I cleared my throat. This felt like one of those nightmares where I was the star of the school play and it was opening night, only everyone forgot to tell me and I hadn't even *seen* a script. "Well, you know, it ought to be Lady O. For O'Brian. Or Lady O. B. Or . . ." When everyone in the car turned to look at me, my voice grew soft. "Lady B is fine."

At least eight of us packed in like sardines. Once the last of the doors shut and we pulled away from the curb with a squeal of tires, it was impossible to see anyone in the darkness. But Antonio introduced his friends to me anyway, and I immediately forgot them all. Seriously. The guys all had names like X or Raid or Dr. Dedd that sounded like roach sprays, and their girls all sounded like Charmaine or other brands of toilet paper. That one name I remember, because Raid or Wipe Out asked me if I thought Charmaine had a slammin' body. "Naw, don't be disrespectin' my lady," Antonio complained, grabbing my hand and putting it in his lap. That horrified me for a minute, but when I realized he was merely holding it and keeping it well away from the Bad Places zones, I relaxed a little. "Yeah yeah yeeeeeeee-ah," he said, tapping on the driver's shoulder. "Kick it up a notch."

When the driver leaned over to triple the volume on the sound system, DDT or X yelled, like Emeril, *"Bam!"*

It was the last word I heard for a few miles. At the volume we were enduring, I was half-convinced it was the last word I'd be able to hear all evening. This was so the opposite of what I'd been imagining since I'd hung up the phone that afternoon. I thought the first meeting would be a little intimidating, but I'd pictured, you know, just the two of us. And quiet. And talking. Maybe a little bit of lip action at the end. I didn't know there would be peeps. I felt like I was caught in some bad Eminem video. Were all dates like this? They couldn't be. And how were they going to scrub the bloodstains from my exploding eardrums off the genuine leather interior?

When we finally pulled to a stop twenty minutes later, my neck and arms were cramped from being squished in the back with so many people, my head was throbbing, and I had resigned myself to death by suffocation from eight different colognes and perfumes. The door opened, and after one of the squeezably soft toilet paper girls and one of the insecticide guys crawled out onto the sidewalk, I clawed my way across the pimpmobile after them.

Once I'd unbent a few dozen joints I never knew I had and the ringing in my ears receded a little, I felt much more talkative—and apprehensive. "Where are we?" I genuinely wanted to know. Soho? It wasn't any part of Soho my dad ever let me visit. All up and down the dark street hulked old warehouses. They all had bars and grates and iron shutters pulled over their doors. Only a few carried signs that gave any indication what they might be by daylight. There was only one working light illuminating the entire street, and it was nearly half a block away. I didn't recognize the names on the street signs overhead, either.

Antonio was the last one out of the car. He patted it on its long magenta trunk to let the driver know he could pull away, and I watched the orange and yellow flames vanish into the murk with a sense of doom. How was I going to get a cab out here in the middle of nowhere, if I had to make a quick getaway? His peeps hung around in silence while he sauntered up to my side and put his arm around me. It would have been more impressive if the fabric of his bright white sweat-suit hadn't shimmered like something radioactive. "Someplace fun, Lady B," he said. "You'll like it."

The tattered awning over the door read TH WIG F CTORY. "We're buying wigs?" I said nervously. Once again, my radar was seriously pinging. The place looked like a crack house. It's hard to explain . . . it's not like any of these Charmaines or Snuggles or Raids had made a move to hurt me, or that they had said anything mean, or even that this Wig Factory place was any scarier than some of the weird art galleries that Jasmine had dragged me to over the last three years. I knew that right then I didn't want to be on this date, that it wasn't anything like I expected, and that I wished—oh, I don't know. I wished I didn't feel like the star of an HBO family special about a teen girl who meets an unfortunate end in an inner-city drug den.

"Nah, this is my favorite hangout, right y'all?" The distant streetlight cast long shadows from the peeps in my direction. I could see that they knew I wasn't like them. It wasn't only superficial differences either, like my timid little white private school girl clothing next to their rap video extravaganzas. I was practically an alien species. They nodded grudgingly at his question. "So it's cool. Don't worry, dawg."

I nodded. What choice did I have? Run down the street like a crazy girl and hope that I met a mugger before a rapist found me first? Antonio laid his hand on my shoulder and his peeps lined up—some in front, some behind—like the two of us were royalty and they were our lords and ladies in waiting.

I didn't hear the music until we were past the second of the Wig Factory's doors. And it wasn't music, really. It was rhythm, pure and simple. Drums and voice. We rounded the corner of the corridor and spilled out into a room that hadn't been painted since the building had been built, roughly in the Mesozoic era; powdery piles of plaster lay under the spots where the ceiling had caved in; the walls looked as if they were covered with mold. Most of the room was taken up by a raised platform where an older man sat, his skin brown and his braids laced with gray, with a yard-high drum between his thighs. A younger guy stood at the microphone, spitting rhymes into it in a raplike rhythm. All around the stage were crowded tables and chairs, each one lit with a fat candle. Somehow it felt almost homey.

And Antonio was the king of the place. The minute he walked in, heads turned. It was as if he gave off some unidentifiable electrical charge that everyone recognized. The drummer raised one hand to his forehead to give a salute from across the room; the couples at the tables murmured to each other and turned their heads in our directions. Even though I couldn't read his expression with those enormous sunglasses still on—and nothing brighter than a ten-watt bulb hung from the flaking ceiling—it seemed to me that Antonio enjoyed the attention. He stood there for a minute while removing his oversized leather letter jacket, then let everyone observe the perfect whiteness of his velour sweatsuit. "Yo," he finally said, once

133

he'd sucked up all the energy from the curious crowd. "Let's chill, y'all."

He grabbed my hand and pulled me in the direction of a table to the side, a little larger and more comfortable than the others. "What kind of place is this?" I asked, looking at the counter at the far end of the room, where girls in skimpy skirts and vests poured hot drinks into mugs. I was relieved it probably wasn't a drug den, but I still felt way, way out of my element. "Like, a hippie hangout?"

Antonio looked at me like I was crazy. "It's a poetry bar, B." The peeps all laughed at me. I hated feeling like I'd hatched from an egg moments before. How was I supposed to know? "It's where I come when I gots to be keeping it real."

"Oh." We sat down on a bench against the wall, where we could see the rest of the room. On stage, the guy behind the microphone shifted into a different rhythm. He wasn't rapping, exactly—the words were more heavily accented, and he seemed to be acting out his emotions with his free hand as he kept sputtering out the words.

> "So I took you to your place
> And I asked you for your name
> Then you walked me to the door
> And you said you knew my game.
> A playah?
> No way, I
> Treat you with respect,
> I'd show you off at places where they'd
> Know you was my dame!"

It was kind of fun, and definitely playful. I was almost enjoying the performance and had started to relax a little when someone came up and sat on the table to talk to Antonio. They obviously knew each other. I slid over a little on the bench to give them room. Then a girl came over and occupied Antonio's other side. I slid over a little more. A couple more people crowded in front of me. Pretty soon I was sitting on the bench's very edge, and then when some of the peeps came back with coffee and Italian sodas and began to chat up the people already lavishing Antonio with compliments and attention, I found myself shoved off my perch. I stood up and leaned against the wall nearby.

I guess it shows what kind of fool I am that I lingered there for over a half hour, biting my lip and feeling miserable and lonely. I know celebrities have a duty to their fans. But what about me? They had duties to their dates as well, right? I kept hoping Antonio would eventually tire of people jockeying for his attention—that he'd look around and find me standing meekly against the wall, waiting for him, and smile in my direction. Was I stupid? I so wanted to believe I was worth remembering.

The longer I stood there, though, the more impatient I got with myself. Why in the world was I putting up with any of this? If I'd come to this Wig Factory with Jasmine and her kooky art-fart friends, or if I'd come with my own girls, I really would've enjoyed it. Right then, however, I felt like I was the fifteenth wheel.

I could do two things: I could find a way home on

my own, or I could endure and wait for it all to be over. Enduring would be so easy. I'd grit my teeth and settle in and *bear* it, like I'd done the year before in algebra. If I somehow found a way home on my own, there'd be questions, and consequences, that would be less easy to endure. Man! I really resented Antonio at that moment. He'd put me in this miserable position.

That anger had been enough to propel me to the pay phone in the dank and dirty back hallway. Taryn had been the first person I could think of to call. "There's nothing wrong," I told her, holding my free hand to my ear. "But . . . it's all so *wrong.*" I sounded so lame. "I'll explain it to you later. I have to get out of here. Now."

I heard Taryn whistle. "I'd ask Mom if we could come get you, but you know she'd call your dad before we left."

That was definitely not a scenario I relished. "I don't know what to do!" I said, trying not to sound all self-pitying and whiny. "I don't even know where I am!"

Taryn made a suggestion then that made both perfect sense and yet horrified me more than a three-day slasher movie festival. Let me tell anyone who doubts it for a moment, though, that nothing I imagined was worse than the actual experience of hanging up, punching out Molly's number, and having my sister shriek at top volume, *"WHAAAAAAT?!"*

Yeah, it wasn't a good evening for my eardrums. Not at all.

136

CHAPTER ONE:

~~How can you tell if a boy loves you?~~
~~How can you tell if he's always thinking of you?~~
~~It's in his kiss.~~
(Isn't this a song? Ask Calvin.)

I repeated the cross streets I'd seen before we came into the building. *"Beaner O'Brian!"* she screamed so loudly that I had to hold the phone away from my ear. *"How in the hell did you manage to get yourself to that part of the city after dark?"*

"God, Molly! I was on a date!" I said. When she started squawking again, I added, "So are you coming to get me or should I wait on the street corner to see if I can find a new pimp?" I could practically feel the breeze from her hanging up the phone and running out the door.

When I turned around, one of the toilet paper girls stood behind me with her arms crossed. I think it might have been she of the slammin' body, Charmaine herself. She popped her gum, tossed her blond hair, looked me up and down, and raised her eyebrow. " 'Tonio is axing where you at."

"He can keep axing," I told her. "I'm going home."

I brushed past the girl and made my way between the empty chairs littering the back of the room, ignoring the crowd of people at the far side where I'd been standing only a few minutes before. This date was officially over.

He found me a little later, where I was standing in the vestibule between the inside and the outside doors, taking peeks outside to see if Molly had arrived yet. I wasn't surprised when he appeared, but I was surprised he was alone. "I've been looking for you," Antonio said.

"Not very hard," I pointed out, not looking at him. "I've been standing here for the last twenty minutes."

"Hey, wait a minute, wait a minute, I couldn't get all anxious 'n' like that. My peeps would think I was whipped."

"Well, we certainly wouldn't want *that.*"

I think my sneer showed. We stood there in silence for a little bit. I got so uncomfortable that I looked outside again for Molly's car. "I can get the Cadillac," he said at last.

"My sister's coming to get me."

"I wanted to show you what I was all about," he said.

"No thanks." I sounded much more bitter than I intended. "I think I saw a lot of what you're about."

My words seemed to frustrate him. "Naw, naw, I'm really not about the superficial. Come on back in."

"No."

138

"Come on!"

"No!"

"Come on!"

How many times was I going to have to say it? Before I knew what was happening, Jasmine's words tumbled out of my mouth. "Yo, boo, you be straight trippin'!"

The phrase was so *stupid,* especially coming from my mouth, that after a shocked pause he started to laugh. I really wanted to join in, but stubbornness and pride kept my jaw clenched. "Go back to your peeps," I finally said. "My sister's on the way." No sooner had the words come out of my mouth than I saw Molly's little red Volkswagen nose its way around the corner . . . and turn the wrong way. "She's here now," I said, feeling relieved. I'd be home soon. "So . . . thanks for a nice evening."

Lame, lame, lame. Even he wasn't buying it. "Take me with you," he said. It was the last thing I'd expected out of his mouth. "Come on," he said, and for the first time that evening he took off his sunglasses. His eyes were brown and sweet in the dim light of the vestibule, and the corners of his lips tipped up into a smile. "You aren't diggin' it, I—" He couldn't finish the sentence. "Take me with you."

Down the street, my sister had figured out her mistake and was involved in a complicated three-point turn to get her Beetle pointed in the right direction. "I don't want to take Antonio with me." I watched his face fall at the words. "But Eugene can come."

I didn't think he'd do it. I honestly didn't think he'd do it. After a moment, though, he folded his shades and stuck them in the breast pocket of his hooded sweatshirt. "Eugene's kind of boring." His voice had changed; it sounded less sure of itself, less cocky. And definitely less fake streetwise.

"Eugene's the guy I first met."

He hesitated, then reached up and pulled off his big woolen cap. Even though I already knew that beneath it lay blond waves, it was still a little unnerving to watch the dreadlocks disappear into his pocket with the hat. Then he did something I hadn't expected—he tugged at the long, sculpted sideburns running down his jaw and peeled them off as well. He ran his fingers through his hair and gave me a sheepish look. "Better?"

"Much." It was funny: Without the costume and props he was a totally different person. Not merely in the way he looked, but in the awkward way he stood, and the way he seemed to deflate within his clothing. He looked like a little boy dressed up in his older brother's hip-hop streetwear. "What about those peeps of yours?"

Eugene looked back over his shoulder. "Aw, they'll be all right. Mastah Blastah'll be around with the Cadillac to get them home."

Mastah Blastah. What a name! "It's a little crazy, isn't it, running off and not letting them know?" I peeked out through the door and saw my sister's face peering through the windshield, white and worried.

He pulled back the door and gestured to me. "Maybe I'd rather do something crazy with you than hang out with them."

I left the Wig Factory with my shoulders back and my head held high, Eugene following behind. For the first time that evening, I actually felt good about myself.

For some reason Molly had tied a scarf to her head before coming out, and when I opened the back door, I could have sworn she'd come in her pajamas. Her look of concern lasted for as long as it took for the both of us to crawl into the backseat. *"Do you know how much you scared me, Beaner, you little turd-cake!"* she yelled the minute the door was closed. The tires squealed when her lead foot suddenly went down. We pulled away from the curb at roughly the same speed as the lead car in the Indy 500. *"What's with this family tonight? It's absolute chaos! I know that neither Dad nor Jasmine can keep you under control, but if you think I'm going to come running every time you're in one of your messes, you've got another thing coming! Who are YOU?!"*

It took us a minute to realize the question had been directed at Eugene. "An—gene," he gulped. "Eugene." Then to me, "Beaner?"

"It's a nickname. I hate it. Cheese-o-petes, Molly," I complained, fastening my seat belt. Molly drove like a crazy person. I might have been safer taking my chances with the muggers and rapists. We turned off one scary street onto another. "Since when have I asked you to rescue me before?"

"Don't pretend you don't remember when you were eight and we went to Uncle Shannon's farm for my birthday and you climbed the apple tree outside and I tore my *birthday dress* to get you down!"

"Oh, right," I made sure I sounded as sarcastic as possible. "That was on the tip of my tongue. That thing when I was *eight.*" I let it sink in. That was the best she could come up with? "Eugene's my date. Eugene, this is my sister, Molly."

"Dad didn't let me date until I was sixteen," she snapped. I saw her peering back at us in the rearview mirror. "What kind of guy takes a girl to the warehouse district, anyway?"

I opened my mouth to answer, but to my surprise Eugene beat me to it. "I wanted to show Hannah this cool performance space where they do street poetry," he said. I'd been almost afraid that if he talked, it would be as Antonio, but with his hat and glasses off, Eugene dropped the *yo yo yo dawgs* and spoke like a normal person. "That's how I got started," he said to me. "Marty discovered me doing street poetry at a coffeehouse."

"I suppose I've got to take you home too," Molly complained. "I'll probably have to drive out to Hackensack, right?"

"Nah, I only want to make sure Lady . . . Hannah makes it home. I can get a cab from there." In the passing glow of the streetlights, I could tell he was regarding me with smiling eyes. It made me feel all funny.

It was the sort of answer that would placate most parents or just about any crazy sister who put the *loco* in *in loco parentis,* but she kept grumbling to herself in the front, cursing when we finally turned onto a numbered street and headed back in the direction of home. Eugene leaned over, close enough that I could feel the warmth of his breath against my ear as he spoke. "Is she always this . . . ?" He looped a finger around his ear.

"What are you two whispering about back there?" Molly demanded.

"I was telling Eugene that you're about to get married," I improvised.

"Don't even start about that. I'm so *sick* of talking about the wedding! I'm sick of Anas wandering around with his arms hanging by his side like a big baboon, and we had Faris moping around the apartment for some reason or another all evening, and Jasmine making a nuisance, and there's stacks of boxes and lists all over the place, and one of these days real soon I am going to take them all, including Anas and Faris, and throw them off the balcony and hope that fourteen stories is *too high for anything to survive.*"

"Aw, it's only nerves," Eugene said. "My sister was like that when she—"

I covered my ears just in time to partially mute Molly's response. *"I'm sick and tired of people telling me it's only nerves! If this is nerves I want to be nerveless! I want to rip every nerve out of my body! I'm sick and tired of everyone telling me—"*

Yeah, so Eugene got introduced to the O'Brian family in style. One sister who walks out on his date, another who makes him go deaf. Very classy. Once Molly was wound up, it sometimes took hours for her to run out of steam. Her mouth was like a nuclear-powered complaint generator with a half-life of thousands of years, and listing all her problems kept it busy from the dark and dismal streets where we'd started all the way to the nice, bright entryway of my building. We covered Anas, the in-laws, Dad, and even my own inadequacies in such detail that I was sure Eugene would hit the ground running the minute we opened the doors. "And you better believe I'm telling Dad about this, too!" she concluded.

"I'm telling him myself!" I told her, leaning forward. "Listen, seriously, Molly, if there's anything I can do for you guys . . ."

"Oh, whatever," she snapped. "Like you could. Don't let this happen again, for starters. Well, hi there, Roger!" The last four words were so sugar-sweet that I reeled from the emotional whiplash. When I turned, I saw that Eugene had hopped out of his side of the car and opened the door for me. Behind him, the doorman waved at my sister. "You watch out, Beaner," she growled as I moved to get out of the car. "I know it's my wedding and you're feeling left out, but these transparent ploys for attention are only *pissing me off.*"

The little car disappeared into the night traffic. We listened to it screech away. Only when it was quiet did Eugene speak again. "Your sister is marrying a guy named Anus?"

"Oh, very nice," I said, walking with him to the door. Roger swung it open for us. "Especially coming from someone with a driver named Mastah Blastah. Why, yes, I got rid of all my termites with Mastah Blastah Concentrated Insecticide, why do you ask? And Charmaine. Mr. Whipple, don't squeeze the Charmaine! Do you know, Mastah Blastah takes care of all my infestation prob—"

"Okay, okay!" he said, almost giggling. "I know a lot of that stuff must seem pretty stupid to you. Hey, let me walk you to your door at least."

The offer pleased me. We'd reached the elevator. I pushed the button and said, "What I can't figure out is why you invited me out at all. I mean, I'm not a music video vixen."

I admit that's the kind of statement to which you really want the guy to say, *Yes, you are!* so I was slightly disappointed—but only a little—when he didn't contradict me. At the sound of the bell, we boarded the elevator together and I pushed the number 21. "It's because you were so nice to me when I met you, you know, at your dad's office. All the other guys—in the band, those guys—I'm not so good with girls the way they are. I mean, dang, Scotty's getting all kinds of play every time he flashes those teeth. I wanted a girl to hang out with and you seemed so—" I blushed, anticipating what he might say. "Harmless."

The blush instantly faded. "Harmless?" I said. It was the last word I expected. Or wanted.

"Yeah. You know, easy to talk to, not real threatening, someone I could be friends with. That kind of thing." His eyes pleaded with me not to take it the wrong way.

"The kind of girl you could talk to about other girls? The kind of girl you could tell about the movies you saw?" Eugene nodded. Was he an utter idiot? How could he say those hurtful things to my face and think they were kind? Now I knew what my sister felt like when she began one of her rampages. "What do I look like to you, some kind of *starter girl*? Do I have *training wheels* attached to my *behind* so you won't *fall off?*"

"I didn't mean—"

"That's so sick!" It was with impatience that I

145

watched the numbers change from 8 to 9. "You don't think I'm attractive at all? I'm not the kind of girl you'd mack down on?"

I was frightening him. "You're getting it all wrong."

"So kiss me." Even as I said the words, I knew I was out of control. What was I trying to prove with any of this? I felt like I was cornering him when he backed away from me as I drew nearer. "Come on," I ordered him, pointing to my lips. "Plant one on me. I'll show you how *harmless* I am." When he didn't move, I closed the gap between us.

His head reared back, away from mine. "I'm not into—I'm—!"

Oh, so I was *that* repulsive? I wanted to slap him. Not only him, but every other boy who'd ever treated me like a buddy, a pal. Harmless ol' Hannah. Okay to talk to, not good enough to kiss—good soul in an ugly shell.

Then I stopped. Eugene looked panicked. It wasn't solely my anger that was freaking him out. There was something more, and I hadn't paid attention. I suddenly knew exactly what he had been going to say. It wasn't *I'm not into you.* Not at all.

He had been going to say *I'm not into girls.*

I stepped back, instantly ashamed of myself. "Oh. You mean you're . . . different," I finished for him, hoping he would take it kindly.

"No!" The expression on his face was terrible to behold. His eyes flew open. His jaw dropped. He hugged himself with his arms. At the same time, though, he seemed absolutely relieved that I understood. "Yes. Please . . . don't tell," he whispered. I couldn't believe I'd made him so miserable.

The bell rang. The sound of the heavy metal doors sliding open seemed to underline the silence between us. I felt pity for him right then. Not because of the whole gay thing—I mean, that's like feeling sorry for someone because of their eye color or the way their nose looks. No, my pity was for the kid muffled in ugly velour, the Eugene hiding behind Antonio. It was right then I started to laugh. He looked hurt, as if I was mocking him. "It's got to be hard," I said, punching the button so that the doors wouldn't close. "You talk about keeping it real, but don't you get tired, pretending to be someone you're not? I mean, the clothes, the car, the phony . . . *everything?*"

He shrugged, then nodded. "It's cool, though."

"But it's *not* cool. You're stuck being someone you aren't. You're different and you can't show it."

"Yeah . . . but it's not that bad." He had relaxed some since I attempted to force a kiss on him. "Most of the time, anyway."

"I think it is." I don't know what I expected to accomplish. Was he going to quit the most successful boy band of all time because I told him to throw away the dreadlocks? Doubtful. Not only was he making beaucoups of bucks, but I could tell he loved the attention he got when he was full-on Antonio. Would I give up all that because someone pointed out I wasn't entirely real?

The poor guy was in a difficult place. "I'm sorry," I said to him, putting a hand on his cheek. The elevator door slid shut when I let go of the button, but we didn't go anywhere. "I'm sorry we had an *awful* evening, and I do mean awful. I'm sorry I didn't fit in with your friends. Most of all, I'm sorry I can't be a make-believe girlfriend."

"I never—I really did like you, Hannah. It wasn't just that."

"You threatened not to do that 'XTreme Video Request' appearance Monday!"

"Nah, that was Marty, not me. Honest. I liked you, and kinda wanted to be friends." When he twisted his foot, he looked much younger and more awkward than he really was.

"We'll be friends," I told him. I'm not sure what it was that made me do it, but I pulled his face to mine and pressed my lips to his cheek. "But man, for the trouble I'm going to be in after this, you owe me *big time*. I'm talking front row tickets to your concerts for me and my friends *and* backstage passes. Or I'm going to sic Molly on you."

"Yo, don't be scarin' a brother like that!" he said, dropping back into Antonio for a second. Then he grinned. "Okay, okay, I promise. You're a pretty cool girl, Hannah."

I pushed 21 again and listened to the door whir open. When I stepped off the elevator, after kissing the tips of my fingers and waving them at him, I felt years older than when I had stepped on.

Dad was waiting for me on the living room sofa, lit only by the light from the kitchen that had been on when I left. His arms were crossed and his face in shadow. "You're a half hour late," he told me in a voice drained of emotion.

"I know."

"Molly called and told me everything."

Ugh. "Yeah, I figured she would."

Instead of the lecture I expected, accompanied by fireworks and musical accompaniment by hell's marching band, he only sighed. "You're not hurt, are you?"

"No, Dad."

"You didn't let him . . . he didn't make you a woman, did he?"

"Dad!" I gasped, appalled. When he didn't respond, I plopped down on the cushion next to him. How long had he been sitting there, all by himself? "Where's Jasmine?"

"She left."

"You guys fought? She'll be back tomorrow."

"I don't know," he said. "She said some pretty harsh things. Harsh for her."

"Sorry." Last year when they had their big annual blow-out, Jasmine had stormed off and spent a night at Molly's. They'd had a mad passionate makeup session the next day. Oh. Maybe that's why Molly had been complaining about Jasmine, and family chaos. Small wonder Molly had been such a crab. I would be too, with Jasmine and Anas and Faris around my apartment. . . .

Oh, *no!*

I let loose with a swear word I usually don't say in front of family.

"What, a single date and you think you're allowed to cuss in front of your father?" He slumped back into the cushions. "Aw, jeez. The hell with it. I don't feel like working up a lather." He said the word himself, then repeated it three times for emphasis. "We'll be okay, honey. Don't worry."

"I know, Daddy." It felt good to be in his arms, just the two of us, and to smell the familiar scent of what was left of his aftershave, but I hadn't been cursing because I was worried about Dad.

It was Faris. I'd completely, utterly, *stupidly* forgotten about the date I'd promised him.

CHAPTER ONE:

Okay, let's face it. Boys pretty basically suck.

Mrs. Aloul seemed awfully surprised to see me standing at the bottom of her front stairs. In fact, she stared at me bug-eyed, as if I was a talking Mrs. Potato Head wearing high heels and a muumuu. Did she dislike me or something? It was difficult to tell. I knew she worked as a translator for the UN, so surely a kid in shorts and a T-shirt and flip-flops at her front door on a Sunday morning wasn't the weirdest thing she'd ever seen. Finally her lips worked and she said, like she was dredging the name from some distant cubbyhole in her brain, "Hannah? O'Brian?"

I hoped she was suffering from one of those remember-the-face, don't-remember-the-name moments and really wasn't horrified to see me. "That's right! Hi! How are you!" I said, trying to sound as cheerful as possible. My words came out so zippitydoodah Mouseketeer merry that I sounded either like a deranged lunatic or a really happy Mormon missionary. I toned it down a notch. "Is Faris around?"

"I'll see," she said, still a little bewildered. "Won't you come in?"

The Alouls lived in an old brownstone on the Upper East Side with a lower floor entrance—one of those streets that production crews use whenever they want to make a film where all the women wear bustles and the men don top hats, and everyone rides around in romantic carriages pulled by horses. The kind of movie, in other words, that my dad will see and afterwards say, " 'Masterpiece Theatre' puked up again." The brownstone's outside was all stately, classical architecture and wrought ironwork, but inside was sleek and modern, where white walls displayed abstract paintings and offset sleek, shiny furniture. I'd been there twice before, when the Alouls and the O'Brians had thrown engagement party shindigs, and both times I'd been terrified of touching anything and leaving greasy fingerprints. I stuck to the sisal runner in the middle of the hallway. We paused by the stairs. "I'll pop upstairs and see if he's . . ." The top wood stair rang out like a gunshot as someone stepped on it. Someone's shiny black shoes began the descent.

"Hey, Ma, what's for—Hannah?" What gave the Alouls the right to look so *good* at nine in the morning? Anas's eyebrows were smoothed, his goatee was neat and trimmed, his hair was tousled perfectly, and he wore a spanking white dress shirt casually hanging outside his ironed jeans. I mean, jeez, Mrs. Aloul wore a perfectly draped sari, running shoes, and a turban and even with the sneakers she still looked ready to attend some embassy party. Mr. Aloul was probably upstairs brushing his teeth in a tux. "What are you doing here?"

Mrs. Aloul gave her older son a smile, a pat, and a smooch on the cheek as she passed him on the way up. "There's French toast for you in the oven," she said. What a mama's boy! He was going to have one heck of a surprise if he thought Molly would be bringing him breakfast in bed. Wait—if they'd been shacking up, he already knew what a crab she was in the morning.

Wait—if they were living together, why in the world was he here, at his parents' house, wearing that Zestfully clean scent and hunting down breakfast? "Why aren't you at home?" I asked him.

He cleared his throat and said loudly, "I had to get to work this morning, so—"

"On a Sunday? What's going on?" I hissed at him.

His head jerked to see if his mother was out of earshot. "Hey, keep it quiet, will you?" he complained.

"What are you doing here? Why aren't you at Molly's?"

He grabbed my arm and pulled me into the kitchen, which smelled like coffee and vanilla and resembled a spread from a gracious living magazine. "I sublet my old apartment, so this was the only place I could go." When I made the there's-some-missing-link-here face, he added, "After Molly threw me out."

"She threw you *out?* What did you *do?*"

For a second I thought he was going to run his hands through his hair, but I guess Pomade Central was a don't-touch zone. Instead, he started digging through a candy jar. "Do! I didn't do anything! After Jasmine showed up last night they shared a couple of bottles of Merlot and started giggling and yelling about how terrible men were. Then Molly threw up on the hearth rug and told me to get out. Your sister is crazy," he accused, as if I'd been the one to make her that way.

"You think I don't know that?" I practically yelled. When he suddenly straightened up from his slump and removed his hand from the candy, I realized that his mother was walking up softly from behind. "So, yeah, I *love* my pillow-mint bridesmaid's dress," I said in my phony Mouseketeer voice. "It's . . ." *Dreary* came to mind. So did *dreadful*. What came out was, ". . . dreamy!"

Was I making everyone else as ill as I made myself? Very likely, because Mrs. Aloul tried to look very kind as she put a hand on my elbow. "I'm afraid Faris isn't, well, here," she said.

"Oh. Okay. Where is he?"

I recognized the question as intrusive the moment I asked it. "He's at work."

"On a Sunday?"

Mother and son swapped a pair of glances. I could tell by their pressed lips that Mrs. Aloul was lying. The whole family was a pack of liars, with Mrs. Aloul covering for Faris and Anas lying to her about his living situation. At least it wasn't only us O'Brians. "I'm sorry if I seemed startled when I saw you outside, my dear," she said, herding me to the door. "I wasn't expecting visitors so early in the morning. But of course you're welcome anytime. You know that, don't you?" We were back in the hallway by that point. I tried to get a word in edgewise but failed. She was simply too determined. "We're practically family, after all."

All that was probably a big fat lie, too. "Could you at least tell Faris I was here?" I asked.

"Of course, dear. Do come again!" I must've felt bad. I let her close the door without even a good-bye. Out in the street, I looked up at the third story. I knew Faris's room faced the street. I thought I caught a flicker of movement behind the curtains, but it was impossible to tell.

Mrs. Aloul might have been fibbing, I reflected on the train, but at least she wasn't a stander-upper, a thoughtless breaker of promises. She at least wore a nice smile when she did her dirty deeds. I was the one who'd stuck the knife in a guy's back and twisted it to the accompaniment of S.W.A.K.

Ever since I'd realized I'd completely forgotten my promise to Faris, I'd felt like an utter turd. Faris was the one person in my life who thought a person's word meant something—and the first promise I'd made to him, I'd abandoned. I mean, total crap-out, no excuses, no alibis. Didn't he once say that Molly and I weren't very different? Maybe we were both oath-breakers. He must think our family was a mess.

Maybe he was right. I'd spent way too much time burying my head in the sand. I'd missed appointments. I'd tried to pretend the wedding wasn't happening. My summer writing assignment languished for so long that now I doubted I'd ever hand in anything. How stupid I'd been! How difficult would it have been to have kept my eyes and ears open? What in the world was I running from? Growing up? Acting like a kid wasn't getting me anyplace but in the Dumpster, and fast.

Maybe I deserved the cold shoulder. Maybe I deserved to be lied to. Maybe I deserved the very worst fate that could possibly befall a girl like me, a girl who'd—

I smelled, before I actually saw, the old man who plopped down next to me. "Hey, girly! Hey, girly! Hey, girly!" he babbled.

Ew. Ew ew ew! I didn't deserve *that*. I contemplated skedaddling away. Aw, screw that. I'd done enough running away. "I know how to shatter a bone with a single blow," I snarled. That was enough to shut his mouth. "Go away. And don't bother me ever, ever again."

Weird thing is—it worked. I'd put up with the Self-Grabber's almost uncanny appearances on my trains on nearly a daily basis for two years. Just the sight of him made my skin crawl. Now, when I watched him jump up and rush into the next car, I knew Mr. Hey Girly would never bother me again.

That felt good. Really good, in fact. My accomplishment made me sit up and straighten my shoulders. People would actually *do* things when I told them to. I'd never before considered such a thing.

I called my dad's cell phone from a tiny Korean convenience store in Brooklyn on my way to Molly's. "Where are you?" he asked. He sounded glum.

"Where are you?" I asked right back. I didn't want to spill my mission quite yet.

"The office." He sighed deeply.

"This is going to be a weird question, but is Faris there?" I asked.

"On a Sunday? You've got to be kidding. No, I'm here by myself. Alone. By myself," he repeated.

That was odd. Okay, the notion that my father would go into the office on a Sunday wasn't at all odd. He went to his office every day of the week. "Where are Fonzi and Calvin?" Sundays they would usually join Dad in the office, and then he'd take them to brunch and come home in the early afternoon.

"Not here." Sometimes, with macho types who never cry, when they're sad their voices take on weight that drags them into hollow depths. I could tell Dad was pretty low. "Apparently Fonzi decided to call in sick. Then ten minutes later Calvin left a message saying he was staying home today. Quite a coincidence, huh?"

I didn't know what he was getting at. "I guess."

"Yeah, real funny how they both *called from Fonzi's home phone.* You'd think they'd remember we have caller ID here!" He said a lot more after that, but the only word that wouldn't make our priest blush was *ingrates.*

"I don't get it."

"They're having some kind of . . . honey, don't make your daddy explain the facts of life to you. They're spending the day together, if they didn't already spend the night."

I felt a flush cross my face. Suddenly the tiny convenience store seemed very hot. "Oh, my God!" I yelled into the phone. "*Fonzi* is his sexy Queen of the Nile?!"

157

Suddenly the store seemed very quiet—probably because three little old Korean ladies and the lesbian couple buying dog kibble had all turned around to stare at me. The Korean lady behind the counter even reached over and shut off her little radio so she could hear better.

"Honey, Daddy doesn't have time to learn slang today," I heard. "It's bad enough with your step . . ." He started to sound sad again.

I turned away from the inquisitive stares and lowered my voice. "Daddy, why don't you meet me at home in a little bit? Jasmine and I would love to go out to brunch with you."

"Your stepmother's not coming home. If that cheating wench did, I'm not sure I'd allow her through the door!" Huh? This was a change from last night. Before I could ask, he added, "I should level with you, Beaner. I found out your stepmother is having an affair."

"My stepmother's having an *affair?*" I repeated, more loudly than I intended. When I looked over my shoulder, I saw the Korean ladies babbling with excitement. "She isn't! She wouldn't! She couldn't!" Blankets were made for hiding on days like this. "Jasmine's not the type. She adores you!"

"Oh ho ho, does she now? Then tell your daddy why, when I was going through the laundry, I found a note from her . . . from her . . . *gigolo?*"

"Jasmine has a gigolo?!" Behind me, one of the lesbians gasped. I shot her a dirty look.

"You betcha. Written on XT letterhead, even. *'Hey, hot stuff,'* it said. *'I've had my eye on you ever since*

158

you walked through my door.' Some disgusting non-sense like that, anyway."

"Oh, no!" I recognized the note. To my utter horror, I realized I'd been the one who left it in Jasmine's sweater. "Dad—"

"That poor girl," said the shorter lesbian.

Her companion nodded and agreed. "Second marriages never work out."

"Probably a rebound match."

Meanwhile, my dad kept ranting. *"'Let's hook up Saturday night,'* it said. No wonder she picked that argument with me. She planned to leave me all along. She doesn't love us, Beaner. I swear to God, I'll find out who's got her now and hunt him down like a dog, even if it takes going through every office in the frickin' building and—"

"Dad, she loves you. Listen to me a minute—no, listen to me." It was impossible to get him to calm down. "Hamilton wrote it. Hamilton Browder. The intern?" He went silent. Before he could get the wrong idea in his head, I added, "He wrote it to Taryn. I was going to deliver it and instead I put it in Jasmine's sweater pocket and forgot." And wouldn't Taryn hate me when I told her what I'd forgotten, too! I mean, no wonder she didn't have anything to do but let me call her last night. Another promise abandoned. What a total cow pie of a friend I was!

That would have to be a hurdle I faced later, though. "Honey, it's nice for you to try to cover up for the no-good, cheating strumpet I married after your mother, God bless her soul, passed on, but it's all right. Your daddy knows that he's going to end his life sad and alone. Your mother's gone. Fonzi and Calvin abandoned me. Jasmine left. Your sister's getting married, and one day you won't love your daddy any more and you'll leave too."

"Jasmine is not a strumpet!"

"Oh, yes she is!" said the lesbians in chorus.

"Would you *pardon me,* please?" I said to them. "Hello? Touching moment between father and daughter? Touching *private* moment?" They turned around, disappointed. "Sheesh. Daddy . . . promise me you won't do anything drastic. I'm not leaving you! I'm heading to Molly's right now to talk to Jasmine. I promise you I'll clear everything up."

"There's nothing you can do, baby. You're only a child."

"And you're a grumpy old man and I love you," I said. "You'll see what a child can do." When I hung up the phone, the little Korean lady behind the counter burst into applause for two seconds, remembered she wasn't supposed to be listening, and then stopped. "I'm never buying gum here again," I told her.

"Little girl, you never buy gum here now!" she snapped. Then the pack of them burst into laughter. Honestly. Waiter? Maturity check, please!

Despite the fact that I knew she usually went to Mass on Sundays, I'd fully expected to find Molly at her apartment. I'd even prepared a half dozen reasons to explain my visit, from, "Hi! I thought you might want some help with the invitations!" to "Molly, what am I going to do with my hair on your wedding day?" By the time I reached the apartment door, though, I'd second-guessed myself so many times that my stomach was tied into knots. The invitations had to be out by now, right? And if Molly and I and the bridesmaids already had some appointment on the day of the wedding to have our hair and makeup done, and I had missed someone telling me, wouldn't my other question send my sister into a hissy? When the door opened in mid-bell press and Jasmine was behind it, my heart nearly stopped.

"Hannah!" Was Jasmine actually glad to see me? She surely looked it as she scanned my outfit. I was even relieved to see her familiar pained look at my footwear. "What *have* I told you about those flop-flops?"

"Flip-flops," I corrected her with a grin. Was it possible I was relieved to see Jasmine too? Was Hell really experiencing a record cold snap? "And yes, I know, they're played out and not phat."

"They're wack," she said. "And they promote nail fungus."

"Jasmine," I said, trying not to bite her, "we need to talk. About you and Dad."

She gathered the folds of her silk robe and turned away from me as she walked to the kitchen. I closed the door behind me and followed. "If I talk about that, I'll wrinkle," Jasmine moaned slightly. On the counter sat a half-finished cup of herbal tea. I remembered what Anas and Molly had done in the kitchen not all that long ago and tried not to touch anything or to think about where they might have done it. "Your father has already given me crow's feet this weekend."

"It's really important," I told her. "Isn't there anything I can do to make you talk?"

She bit her lip speculatively. I recognized the gleam in her eye.

Twenty minutes later I found myself stretched out on Molly's sofa with a mint honey-sugar facial masque oozing its way into every crevice in my skin. For years Jasmine had been trying to get me into a mint honey-sugar facial masque, and for years I'd avoided it. I learned the complete recipe along the way:

1. Take 1 teaspoon of honey and 1½ teaspoons of granulated sugar.
2. Crush a small handful of dried mint leaves with a mortar and pestle. (Me: "Who packs a mortar and pestle in their overnight bag?!" Jasmine: "I do.")
3. Mix thoroughly in a Spode teacup, circa 1785.
4. Moisten the face and throat with imported mineral water from an artesian well.
5. Apply. Scrub gently. Scrub. Scrub. Scrub!
6. Allow masque to remain on the face while you place cucumber slices on your eyes.
7. While the masque is on (but before the cucumbers), make yourself a vodka martini and give your stepdaughter a diet Squirt.
8. Moan gently about your problems.

"So, when are you going back to Dad?" I asked her point blank, once we were on opposite sofas with our faces marinating. "Haven't you tortured him long enough?"

"Your father hasn't called. He hasn't sent flowers. He hasn't even phoned your sister to see if I'm here."

Even with my eyes marinating in salad I could tell she was miffed. "Maybe he doesn't want me to go back."

"You know how stubborn we O'Brians are. And it's really not his fault," I said. The masque kept seeping around my lips. Whenever I licked them, I tasted like baklava. "He thinks you have a gigolo."

My advice to anyone who is tempted to tell their stepmother that her husband thinks she has a gigolo? Don't. They don't take it very well. *"Merde!"* she yelled. "That's idiocy! How did Barry come by so mis-informed an idea? I could *kill* the person who made him think such a thing!"

If I'd been a cartoon character, a little balloon would have appeared above my head then, accompanied by the word *GULP!* "Well . . ." I wondered if I should abandon my cucumbers and head for the hills. What came next took courage. I swallowed and told her the story of how I'd taken Hamilton's note and stuffed it in her sweater pocket and forgotten about it.

There was a moment of silence. "Hannah O'Brian!" I heard her say in the voice of Cruella DeVille. Oh, crud. Here came the fireworks, I just knew it. "I can't believe you put that sweater in the *hamper!* Don't you know all my sweaters go to the *dry cleaners?"*

"Huh?" I started to sit up and remove my cucum-bers. I was sick of this masque thing, anyway.

"Lie back down!" she barked. In my brief glimpse, I'd seen that she was still lying perfectly still with her arms crossed over her chest, like an Egyptian mummy. I obeyed and kept quiet for a moment. If she hadn't been a model, Jasmine would have excelled as a pit bull trainer.

After a moment I heard some small muffled noises from her sofa. They sounded like sobs. "Are you okay?" I asked, afraid to move, but for some strange reason wanting to comfort her.

I shouldn't have worried. As soon as I asked the question the noises erupted into full-fledged laughter. She had been giggling! "Me and a gigolo!" she said. "Oh, that's rich! A gigolo!"

Big buckets of air conditioning on a July afternoon would not have been more of a relief than what I felt at the sound of her amusement. "You're not going to leave him, are you?" I still had to know.

"Oh, Hannah, sweetie," she said. "Do you really care?"

It was a slap of a question, but maybe I deserved it. "Yes." It was embarrassing to admit, but I really did care. Dad loved Jasmine. "Please don't. You're good for him. If it's anything I did—"

"No diggety your father is a pig-headed mofo who *occasionally* gets it into his head that I have no say in your upbringing, and *occasionally* I have to teach him a lesson by reminding him how empty and boring his life is without my influence, but if you think I'd leave him, you're straight trippin'. None of it was because of you."

"It's not true. Everything's my fault!" Damn the cucumbers! I plucked them from my eyes and deposited them in a glass bowl on the coffee table.

"Lie back down," Jasmine said. "Your masque will run."

"I don't care if it runs so much that Winnie the Pooh wants to jump me," I told her. Why did I even bother?

"None of it matters. Everything I touch turns to turds. Dad's running around crazy jealous because you've got a gigolo because of me, you're sleeping here because of me, Anas is sleeping at his mom and dad's because of me, Taryn is dateless, Hamilton is probably pissed, and I've got a boy band member who might not ever have found his pimpmobile or his peeps again for all I know. I've been banned from a Korean market. Faris hates me and won't see me. And Molly's leaving Anas," I added to my long, sad list before I realized what I'd said. Then again, maybe it was better to talk about it. I'd kept the split a secret too long, and it would all come out soon enough anyway. I had never felt sorrier for myself in my life. "I'll be an awful bridesmaid and I'll be kicked out of school when I don't get this summer assignment done." Jasmine had sat up by now. She placed her cucumber slices in the same bowl as mine. I was miserably aware that gravity was dragging my honey-sugar masque down to my neck. It only made me more upset. "And everybody hates me. And I'm going to be in a broken family. After I've already been an orphan! I'll never be loved! And it's *all because of me!*"

The final complaints sounded ridiculous even as they came out of my mouth, but they somehow had sounded pitiful in my head. Jasmine's glistening mouth twitched a little. "You're laughing at me," I said, my lip wobbling dangerously. Silly sounding or not, I felt utterly wretched.

"Sweetie," she said. When she rose to stand up and sit next to me, she arrived with a rush of perfumed calm. "I *am* laughing at you. But you're so dramatic right now that I think you have to be laughing at yourself a little bit too."

"Not."

Before I knew it, I found her arms around me. It felt strange. Minty goo dripped down our faces and onto each other as she stroked her fingers through my hair. "Oh, sweetie. It's all right. You've got the weight of the world on your shoulders, don't you?" I snuffled and nodded against her shoulder. It was thin and I could feel the bones beneath her skin, but it was comfortable at the same time. "You've never let me hug you before," she murmured.

Of course that comment made me feel self-conscious. I pulled away and tried to wipe away some of the tears that had blended with the goo to make a salty-sweet mess. Jasmine tsked. With a washcloth she moistened in the silver ewer she'd brought from the kitchen, she started dabbing away the muck.

"I'm okay," I told her, but I didn't brush away her hands. I did feel better. I'd always read in magazines how unhealthy it was to bottle up emotions. It always sounded mega-stupid to me. Now, though, I felt as if merely naming all the things that had been weighing on me had taken away their pressure. When I'd been hiding from them and pretending they weren't there, they'd been overwhelming. They hadn't gone away, completely, but somehow they all seemed—I don't know. Approachable.

"When I first met your father," Jasmine was saying, "I thought he was the most irritating little man I'd ever met. He was prideful and so arrogant! But oh, he loved you girls so much. I could tell that when he talked about you. So I knew all the bluster only masked something very special about him, and I fell in love with him for it."

"How can you love someone who annoys you at first?" I asked. "That's pretty weird, isn't it?"

"It happens all the time."

"Okay, maybe, but Dad loving me and Molly is a whole different thing from loving someone for real, isn't it?" I blew my nose.

"Hannah, all love is for real. See, I think that if you have it in you to love something inconsequential, even a poem or a song or a painting, you're capable of loving someone to the fullest and having them love you back. We start loving little things when we're young. A stuffed toy or a doll, something smaller than us. And then we build on that. We love our brothers and sisters, our parents, and then we start loving other people. Friends first, and then lovers. Each little love helps us move on to the next, bigger one.

"They're all part of a long chain that can grow all your life, link by link. Your father loves you and Molly so much, just as he loved your mother and mourned her loss. I knew he was the sort of man I wanted to love myself. I can't give up what I feel for him easily," she said, stroking my hair once more. "I'm not going to leave him, sweetie. And as long as you keep adding to your chain, you'll never be unloved."

I liked her image of a chain of love, each link connected to the other. But I was still scared. "Jasmine, I don't understand any of it. How do you know if someone is the *one?* How do you know if he's not?"

"You simply do. Wait!" she added, silencing me before I could protest. "I know that wasn't the answer you wanted. There's no simple formula for love. You can't learn it from a textbook or write it down for someone else."

"You can't?" I thought of my writing project. That didn't bode well.

"Be yourself, Hannah," she said. "You're a good person to be."

"I am?" Her approving nod made me flush with pleasure. "So I should be real, you mean?" She smiled and held my hand in hers. "Okay, but if am, then could you *please* stop using urban slang? I've heard enough to last a lifetime, thank you very much."

She didn't seem offended at all. "Only if you promise to *talk* to me from now on. And if you allow me to prescribe a skin care regimen. You might not think so now, but it's never too early to start a really proper exfoliation and moisturizing routine."

I thought it over. Right at that moment I genuinely liked Jasmine. I liked her a lot, actually. And as much as I hated to admit it, despite a still sticky residue, my face actually felt very soothed and tingly. "Deal." Then I remembered something. "But what about all my messes?"

"Fix them one at a time, sweetie. There's no rush."

That wasn't at all true. "What about Molly and Anas? They're supposed to be married in days!"

I felt taken aback when Jasmine laughed. "Oh, Hannah. Your sister has—" Swear to God, tender Kodak moment or not, I knew that if Jasmine told me Molly had *nerves,* I was going to lunge at her and rip out her epiglottis. I didn't know what an epiglottis was, but

I'm sure I'd get it along with the rest of her innards. "Your sister has so much on her mind she's temporarily lost sight of what the wedding's really all about. She simply needs a reminder of all the reasons she and Anas wanted to spend the rest of their lives together."

"Hel-*lo!*" I cried, thinking of my aborted scheme with the roses. "That's what I've been saying all along!"

Jasmine squeezed my hand. "Trust your instincts. Now, when are you going to tell me about your date? Did you get everything out of it you thought you would?"

"Not unless you count a thank-you and a hand-shake," I told her. She made a little disappointed face at that, and obviously wanted the whole story—but I'd been struck with a sudden thought. "I'll tell you later. After you're back home."

"That might be another day or two. I'm still waiting for your father to ask me back." Stubborn! Maybe we O'Brians had rubbed off on her.

Trust my instincts, huh? Well, I would. I excused myself and borrowed my sister's phone for a few minutes. When I came back after a long call, Jasmine beamed with delight. "Sweetie, you look positively radiant," she told me.

"It's weird," I told her. "I feel like I could do anything right now."

"When you feel like that," she said, leaning forward and mirroring my smile, "you can."

I probably could too. It was amazing how confident I felt from a stupid facial. No, it wasn't just the facial. It had been everything I'd realized that morning, starting with all the mistakes I'd made over the past few weeks. Mistakes could be mended though, right?"

"Where are you going?" Jasmine asked when I stood up from the sofa with sudden determination.

"First I'm going to wash this crud off my face. No offense, but I feel like a Greek pastry. Then—" My words trailed off.

Well . . . then I was going to fix things.

CHAPTER ONE:

What's the key to finding a boy? Maybe it's simply not to look for one. Start by examining yourself. Start by getting real.

The worst part about my second visit to the Alouls was probably the television. Only thirteen inches? What were they, Communists? No, wait. The worst part about my second visit to the Aloul house on my own were the snacks. That candy Anas had been digging around in earlier? It was some kind of weird sesame thing with seeds that got wedged between my teeth.

No, actually, the single worst part about my second call to the Upper East Side was the moment when, after I burst through the front door with a cheery smile laminated onto my jaw, I thought Mrs. Aloul might toss me back out onto the street. "Hi, there!" I leered. Honestly, it was scary. Someone passing by might have confused my teeth with a piranha's.

"Hannah?" asked Mrs. Aloul. She tried to block me

171

from entering, but I was already pushing my way in. "I'm afraid Faris is still busy. Out, I mean. Out. At work. I'm the one who's busy, I mean, with my desserts. . . ."

"Mmmmm, desserts! Oh, you know how you said I was *always* welcome?" I reminded her, sidling my way past her into the entry hall and backing into the kitchen. "Yeah. That was so sweet. I thought I'd take you up on it. You know, hang out until Faris got home. You and me." She looked so horrified that for a minute I was almost offended. What, I want to know, is so bad about the prospect of a little quality Hannah O'Brian time? Then I saw that the kitchen had been turned into a huge restaurant assembly line and felt a little horrified myself. The rehearsal dinner was in only four days' time. I'd forgotten that the Alouls were hosting it at Mr. Aloul's club. And making all the desserts too, apparently. And I'd interrupted! "Yack!" After taking a deep sniff, I recoiled from an enormous bowl of white gook that looked like snowman vomit and smelled even worse. "What is that stuff?"

"That," she said with great dignity, "is goat cheese for the *kanafi.*" Over in the corner of the room, a little old man sat watching Middle Eastern music videos on the tiny television. One Halloween in second grade, our entire class sculpted faces into apples and then baked them until they were shrunken and wrinkly and leathery; the old man's face looked exactly like what I'd pulled out of the oven. "Uncle Muhab? Look, we have a visitor," said Mrs. Aloul with a decided lack of enthusiasm.

He was a scary old man, but I was determined to be

sociable until I could make my break upstairs. "Hi, Uncle Muhab! I'm Hannah!" He stared at me. A bowl was in his lap. When I peeked in, it was full of a browny sort of goo. "What have you got there?" I asked. "Caramel? Looks yummy!" When the old man looked at me, lifted his upper lip, and let a stream of tobacco cascade into the bowl, I backed off. "Oooookay, so it's not caramel."

I felt bad. Mrs. Aloul didn't seem to know why I was there or what to do with me. I hardly knew why I was there myself. I could do something about the what-to-do-with-me part, though. "So, can I help?" I asked.

It was exactly the right thing to say. Her eyes lit up. "You came to help?" she asked. "She came to help, Uncle Muhab! Oh, there's so much to do and the boys won't set foot in the kitchen. . . . We must get you an apron."

Mrs. Aloul went to a lot of fuss to get me properly covered, which at first didn't make a lot of sense, since I wore a T-shirt and she was the one still in the fab silks. After a few minutes, though, when I found myself drizzling syrup over trays of shredded wheat stuffed with goat cheese, I kind of saw the sense of it. Despite having already been drizzled with honey earlier in the afternoon, I actually found the work kind of fun. Mrs. Aloul relaxed once she realized she was getting twice as much done as before. She talked, I drizzled, and Uncle Muhab hummed along with the music videos. At least I hoped it was humming and not a death rattle.

"You're such a dear!" she finally said, when we'd packed the last of the *kanafi* trays into the industrial-sized refrigerator. "You must be such a help to your mother in the kitchen! Oh, I wish I had a daughter!"

I beamed. The only thing I knew how to cook was ramen noodles. Jasmine would sooner allow a mountain lion with a weak bladder use her refrigerator as a litter box than let me help her near the staging area of one of her international culinary experiences. "Molly will be your daughter soon enough, Mrs. Aloul," I sweetly told her, managing not to add, *and good riddance.*

"I don't suppose you'd help me make the *mahlabiyyeh?*" she pondered, seeming doubtful.

"Mrs. Aloul, I would *so* love to help you make the *mahlabiyyeh!*" I lied with vigor.

She beamed like it was Christmas and she'd moments before found a pony under the tree with her name on it. "*Mahlabiyyeh* is Uncle Muhab's favorite. It's easy on his bowels, poor dear. Now, you wait here and keep Uncle Muhab company while I run down to the grocery for cream."

After the door closed, Uncle Muhab and I stared at each other for a hot second, and then I raced out of the kitchen, up the stairs, and through the Alouls' living room, and then up the second flight of stairs to the top floor. At the back of the house, doors to two bedrooms stood open. One of them held a king-sized bed, a woman's vanity, and a large walk-in closet; obviously the adults' boudoir. The other seemed more like a guest room, though from the rumpled sheets I was guessing it was the room Anas was using in his exile.

Across the hall at the front of the house were two closed doors. I knocked at the one I remembered being Faris's room and listened. I thought I heard movement from within. "Are you in there?" I asked. Again I heard some muffled motion. I rattled the door handle, more as a threat than anything else. It proved to be locked. "I know you're in there," I said. "Won't you let me in?"

Silence.

"Listen. I know you think I'm rotten through and through." Still no reply. Part of me was ticked off I didn't get a denial, but the other part of me knew I didn't deserve one. "I know you think I break my promises. And I did break my promise to you. I'm sorry about that."

I heard some strange kind of noise inside. Was he even listening to me? I raised my voice, aware that any moment I'd hear his mom returning with groceries and my one chance would be lost. "I've been downstairs making *kanafi* with your mom for the last hour," I said. I don't know why I wanted him to know that. "Don't you want to come out and see if I did it right?"

Silence. "Fine. Be that way. No, please *don't* be that way. Listen, I don't like you mad at me. I don't know . . . I don't know why I'm here or why I want you to forgive me, but I do. I only know that when I was with you that afternoon in the costume shop and we nearly . . . well, you know. When we nearly kissed." There. I'd said it. I hadn't cared to admit it, but I'd wanted more than anything that afternoon to see how his lips tasted. "Yeah. When we nearly kissed, it seemed more, I don't know. More *real* than anything else I've ever felt. This is embarrassing. Please open the door."

175

Nothing happened. "Okay, maybe I deserve the silent treatment. I admit that. I'm also admitting I was wrong to stand you up. I completely forgot and I'm sorry. Just give me another chance. Please. This time I promise you I won't run or hide or screw it up. I *promise.*"

Still nothing. I wanted to cry. "Okay, so you're mad. Fine. Whatever. But can you at least give me some kind of sign that you've been listening?"

That's when the toilet flushed on the other side. I blinked multiple times, then jumped back as the door opened. Anas stuck his head out. "When did we nearly kiss?"

For a moment I stood there, utterly horrified. Ever heard of the *Hindenberg*? Yeah, well, for a terrible moment I felt like that big blimp, going down in flames. "What were you doing in there?" I yelled, battering him with my hands.

"Number two, if you really want to know." He grinned. Anas must have seen the tears of embarrassment welling in my eyes then, because he took me by the elbow and steered me across the hall into the spare bedroom, where he sat me down on the bed. "Ssssh, ssssh, it's okay," he said softly. "I'm sorry."

"I thought that was Faris's room," I said, utterly miserable. I'd poured my heart out to a man evacuating his bowels.

"I know, and I should have spoken up. His room is the other door."

"He didn't hear a word I said!"

"I wouldn't be too sure of that." He put a finger to his lips and pulled me so that we both peeked out

176

around the door frame. Across the hall I saw a crack of light from the other closed door, as if Faris had opened it in an attempt to hear our conversation. "I think he heard you loud and clear." We settled back down on the mattress.

"Then why didn't he say anything?" I felt doubly ashamed now.

"A man's got his pride, Beaner."

"Yeah, well, so does a woman," I retorted. "And it's not Beaner. It's Hannah."

"Your sister calls you Beaner," he pointed out.

"Beaner is a kid's name. I'm not a kid." It was strange, but it felt good to say that aloud for the first time. For years I'd been hoping that my nickname would simply vanish, and it never had. Maybe this facing-issues thing had its positive side.

"Okay, okay. Hannah." We sat there for a moment. "Anything I can do to help?"

"You can make sure he's at the studio tomorrow afternoon for 'XTreme Video Request,' " I suggested. It was a little coy to make that suggestion. After all, Faris was already going to be at work—but it was Anas I wanted to show. "You've got the week off for wedding preparations, don't you? You can come down to the station?"

"Sure," he said, a little flustered.

"Promise?" He nodded. That might have been a little mean of me, but if Faris got his notions about keeping promises from his family, maybe they had taken with Anas as well. And I needed Anas to be there tomorrow afternoon.

"So . . . my little brother got lucky with an O'Brian,

huh?" Anas grinned and stroked his goatee. "Smokin'!"

"Hel-lo!" I cried, standing up. "He did not! And I'm sorry, but did you open a window? Because my confidentiality flew right out!"

"Sorry, Beaner. Hannah, I mean. Hannah," he added, before I could remind him.

Across the hall, the thin slit of light disappeared as I stepped out into the hallway. Faris's door stood closed to me. "Now come on," I told Anas. "You're going to help your mom with the *mahlabiyyeh.*"

He winced and backed away. "Kitchen stuff?"

"Yeah," I told him. "Kitchen stuff. And not the kind of kitchen stuff that you and Molly do, either. What is *mahlabiyyeh,* anyway?"

"It's a kind of pudding."

"Are you coming?" I asked him, three steps down. "Or do you want me 'accidentally' telling your mom where you've been living for all these months?" I've never seen anyone run faster in the direction of pudding. Not even Bill Cosby.

This self-assertiveness stuff could get addictive. I felt like I was starting with a clean, blank slate.

CHAPTER ONE:
A New Beginning

"Ohmygodohmygodohmygod!" When I rounded the corner from the dressing rooms, my three friends simultaneously pounded me like linebackers going after their first Superbowl rings. I had no choice but to fall backward under their weight. Thank goodness the "XTreme Video Request" set is mostly made up of retro shag carpet and oversized neon-colored pillows. I guess shag is "in" again, which should give my Aunt Bernice a reason to rejoice. She's been hanging on to her orange carpet for thirty years now. When the show's on the air and filled with kids carefully selected from the crowds milling around the outside doors, it's supposed to look like everybody's hanging out in someone's bedroom. You know, someone with a bedroom that seats fifty people and has a stage. "I so totally can't believe you got us in for this!" squealed Mandy, in my ear.

"Ow!" I complained. "Deafen much?"

"Guys," Carrie said, remembering that she was allegedly big on dignity these days. "We have to stay cool, like everyone else." The older teens and twenty-somethings trying to find places already stared at us as if we'd escaped from the Mad Cow disease quarantine pens. "We're not babies." She settled herself on the edge of an oval cushion, face aloof, knees together, ankles crossed, and flipped her hair over her shoulder. A single photograph of her in the dictionary could easily have defined the word *blasé*.

"Okay." Taryn settled down beside her in exactly the same pose and stared off into space. "Here's what I'll do when S.W.A.K. is on stage." She yawned slightly and tapped the tips of her right fingers against her left palm, as if she was the Queen of England applauding at a garden party.

"Oh, you guys are too much," said Mandy. She settled down between them, threw back her hair, and sat erect with both feet touching the top of the ledge beneath. "Here's what I'll do when they've finished their set." She applauded even more daintily than Taryn and whispered, "Bravo. Bravo."

"Pip pip, old chaps." Taryn nodded graciously, cupped her hand, and rotated it at the wrist in a regal wave.

"You guys are *so* immature." Come to think of it, Carrie's expression would have illustrated the word *scorn* pretty well too. "Don't be wigging out when they show up, like you did at the 'A.M. USA' concert, either."

"Oh, nice!" Taryn settled back into a more comfortable position. The room was really filling up quickly. My friends had chosen a space midway back, toward the side, where they could see the stage unobstructed by cameras. Overhead on the oversized monitors, the XT logo spun endlessly against a blue background. "You were worse than any of us!"

"Really? I don't recall."

Mandy made a face. "We-we? I don't we-kwall!" she mimicked.

I couldn't help but laugh. "I love you guys," I said as I rose to my feet and dusted myself off.

"Where are you going?" Taryn asked. "It's starting in five minutes!" She seemed genuinely concerned I was leaving—which was a relief, since I'd told her about my mistake with Hamilton only that morning. I wouldn't have been surprised if she'd given me the silent treatment. Maybe, though . . . just maybe, judging by the way she was exchanging smiles with an older boy who'd sat down cross-legged next to us on the ledge, she hadn't been all that serious about Hamilton to begin with.

"I'll be back," I told them. "I have to see a few people first."

Molly and Jasmine stood at the set's very edge. Molly in sensible Capris, Jasmine in . . . well. Words fail me. Picture a skin-tight patent pleather catsuit the exact shade of a plastic lawn flamingo, shiny as a rain slicker, with no sleeves or shoulders, laced up in the middle like a bustier. Put a pleather cap of the same color on top of her head, with Jasmine's long black hair cascading down to her butt. Then put some ginormous shades with deep pink frames on her face.

What do you have? A centerfold model from a dirty magazine stuffed under the Pink Panther's mattress.

"You look sixteen," I told her. Jasmine preened, seeming to think it was a compliment. I'm not sure I intended it that way.

Molly managed to look both bored and furious. "And the reason we're here is . . . ?" she snapped at me.

"I told you, dear," said Jasmine. "We're here to see Hannah's new boyfriend." She smiled and nodded at me.

"Not so much," I said. "But something like that. You guys okay over here? You don't want to sit down?"

"The grip told Jasmine the lights reflecting off her outfit would burn out the cameras." From her smirk, I could tell Molly enjoyed that one. Then, as if realizing something, she added, "Beaner's boyfriend plays in a band? Eugene? That weird little geeky guy?"

"Who's Eugene?" Jasmine asked. "She's seeing Antonio. The *A* in S.W.A.K."

"Beaner, exactly how many guys are you dating?"

"One too few." I sighed. I'd clear up all the confusion later, I promised myself. I didn't have much time now. "Molly, if I do you a favor, will you do me one?" I asked her.

She seemed suspicious. "What?"

"If after this I spend the next three days totally devoted to making your wedding the happiest day of your life, including wearing that pillow-mint green bridesmaid's dress without complaint, will you stop calling me Beaner? I want to be Hannah from now on."

Molly pursed her lips. I knew she wouldn't have an answer for me, not then. Later, though, I hoped she would remember the request and maybe honor it. If not, I'd ask again. And again. And again, until it took. Beaner was a kid's name. Hannah was in charge from here on out. I let Jasmine kiss me on the cheek before I moved on.

I passed Aaron Grady right as the "XTreme Video Request" music started blaring over the loudspeakers overhead. He rushed in from the wings where all the stage personnel hovered, ran by without a look, and bellowed into his microphone, "Yeah, boy-ee, it's time to give it up for the hottest videos around!" When I turned around, everyone was applauding. Across the room, halfway up the broad, stacked ledges, my friends craned their necks to see the stage. They were clapping wildly but trying to remain cool and calm. I was very proud of Mandy for not screaming.

This was it—the big moment I'd envisioned. Three weeks ago if the devil had told me I could be here to-day in the XT studios, watching this show in person, and that all I had to do was sell him my soul, I would have pricked my thumbs and shouted, "Where do I sign?" Now here I was, walking away from it all. I was going to skip everything. I'd miss the videos. I'd miss Aaron Grady's interviews with the audience. I was go-ing to miss S.W.A.K., unplugged and live, on the stage not ten feet from where I stood.

And you know what? I was okay with that. I had amends to make.

Anas stood backstage in the near-darkness, waiting

right where I'd told him. "Faris is upstairs," he told me. "Is that what you wanted?"

I nodded, then pointed through the mass of set debris and the crowd of heads. "See that shiny thing over there, the one that looks like a pink Mary Kay lady met an oil slick? That's Jasmine," I said. "There's a commercial break coming up in about thirty seconds. When it does, go stand with her. Molly's there."

That information made him stammer. He rubbed his hand over his face. "What if Molly doesn't want me to—?"

I didn't have time for argument. The commercial break was approaching quickly. "Do you love my sister?" He nodded at my question. "Do you still want to marry her?" He nodded once again. Even in the darkness I could see the sincerity in his eyes. "Then what're you standing here for? Trust me on this one. Okay?" The audience broke into applause. "Go!" I ordered.

He went. So did I, without looking back. In a few more minutes, my plan would be in place.

"Honeybun, what're you doing out here?" Dad wanted to know, out in the hallway. He'd moments before finished talking to the man I recognized as Marty, the manager for S.W.A.K., but he walked past me without any sign of recognition. Dad put a hand to my cheek, baffled. "Are you sick? If you think that just because I relaxed my standards one time so that you could get into the broadcast, I'll let this become a habit, you've got another thing coming, young lady. This is a one-time happening. Oy. Sweetheart, you're too young—"

All the old arguments came bubbling up, one after

the other. I recognized every one. He'd be selling me off to a walrus-eating Siberian again, next. I nearly laughed. "I'm fine," I said. "That is, I have a little headache. I thought I'd see if Fonzi had some aspirin or something."

"Aw, baby, Daddy's sorry," he said, his tone changing so abruptly to genuine regret that I felt bad for deceiving him. "Want I should wait here to let you back in? Better yet, I'll go upstairs with you. I was going to make sure none of those hoodlums, excuse the expression, pulled any crapola, but your health is more . . ."

"Oh, I'll be all right. Molly's inside," I told him. "She was asking for you. She said, and I'm quoting here, that she wanted you to 'be with her.' "

Dad seemed pleased at that, but then stopped. "Wait a minute. I thought I saw you-know-who with her." I raised my eyebrows. "That Woman."

"Jasmine's with her, yes," I told him. I hoped he wouldn't notice I was using the same firm tone he used with me when I was being childish. "But Molly seemed so . . . I don't know. She said that this would be one of the last times she got to do something with you as your child, rather than another man's wife." I turned on the old daughterly charm as I talked. "It seemed real important to her, but I guess if you're too busy being miffed, she'll understand. I mean, it's not like Molly carries grudges or anything." The last part, of course, we both knew to be a blatant lie.

With a puff of his cheeks, Dad blew out a sigh. "I guess I can be the bigger man here." Um, okay, but exactly who was the smaller man? Jasmine, maybe? "After all, she *is* my only daughter."

"Hey!" I protested, dropping all pretense of a headache.

"Sweetie, honey, I mean the only daughter I'll be losing anytime soon. Right?"

"Yeah, nice recovery there, old man," I grumped. "Dad . . . be nice to Jasmine. She really loves you, you know."

He had already turned, however, to investigate his own reflection in a narrow window set into a nearby door. "How's my hair look? What's left of it. Ay yi yi, your daddy's beginning to look like a cue ball, baby. When I'm a senior citizen you can save on the old folk's home by renting me out to a billiards parlor." Dad kissed me on the forehead. "You go get some aspirin. You know what to tell the studio hands to get back in?"

" 'I'm Barry O'Brian's daughter and if you don't let me in he'll have your ass on a plate,' " I parroted. As if I was ever going to be so dorky as to use that. I watched him smooth his hair again and adjust his shirt.

"Oh, well. She'll have to take me as I am, right?"

I knew he wasn't talking about Molly.

A few XT staffers still walked around this late in the afternoon, but the studio halls were largely quiet. I navigated my way to the stairwell, up to the level above, and across to the north end of the building, where my father's office sat. The door stood ajar. When I pulled it open and stepped in, for a startled moment I thought it was deserted.

Then I saw what was going on over by the coatrack. "Ew," I commented, making a show of covering my eyes. "Three words: Get. A. Room. At least *I* know how to count," I added when Calvin glared at me. Fonzi jumped at the sound of my voice, straightened her skirt, and had the decency to keep her eyes low and her cheeks red as she scurried back to her desk. "Don't stop swapping spit on my account," I told them.

"Child, you have got the worst sense of timing Calvin thinks a body could have. Can't a man kiss his lady in private?" The singer's voice sounded deeper and more grumbly than usual.

"Yuh-huh! He sure can! Private! Not in an office lobby!" Calvin narrowed his eyes and glared at me, a move I mirrored. Fonzi, in the meantime, cleared her throat extravagantly and tried to pretend that seconds before she hadn't been allowing Dr. Desburnes, M.D., to perform an exploratory tonsillectomy with the tongue-o-scope. "You adult types kill me," I said, grinning. "Whatever. Get on with it. Is . . . in there?" I gestured to my dad's office and whispered the last question to Fonzi so I couldn't be overheard. She nodded but still refused to look me in the eye. "Great. Proceed. Don't do anything I wouldn't do." Once I was behind Fonzi's back, I turned around and mimed to Calvin while I mouthed the words: *seventy-five bucks!* He still owed me! A pained expression crossed his face as he shooed me off. Fonzi caught the gesture and began to turn around, but I ducked into the office before she could catch us.

Faris sat in my father's chair, staring out the window. The television softly played the number-three video by

Tossing Guppies. At the sound of the door closing, Faris swiveled around and faced me for the first time in two days. *Say something,* I thought to myself, though for the life of me I couldn't tell whether I meant him or me.

I'd really thought a lot about what I planned to say right at that moment. I'd lost sleep over it the night before. I wanted my speech to be elegant. I wanted to sound like a girl at the end of a movie, telling the guy that he had her at hello, or saying she's just a girl standing in front of a guy and asking him to . . . well, not to despise her quite so much. I wanted to say the absolute right thing. Faris stared at me, though, those impossibly bristly eyebrows poking out in every direction, his lips screwed into a scowl, and his dark eyes refusing to budge from mine. All I could think of to say was, "I am such a doof."

He didn't disagree. In fact, he didn't say a word. He simply held the tips of his fingers together as if he was about to demonstrate how to make a church and then a steeple, and stared at me.

I cleared my throat and tried again. "I'm a total idiot."

Instead of answering, he kept gazing at me without a waver. His legs pushed the chair so that it swiveled gently from side to side.

Oh, man, he wasn't making my apology any easier. The only thing I could do was take a deep breath and plow on. "Listen, I know you're mad that I stood you up. I know it was crazy—insane, really—and I shouldn't have done it. It probably won't make you feel better, but I had a hecka-lousy date that night, and oh . . . whatever. There's probably nothing I can do to make it up to you."

188

Nothing? There ought to have been something. Right? Surely he could think of a contradiction? Still, he kept silent.

"Oh, come on!" I stamped my foot, and immediately felt bad for losing my temper. "I embarrassed myself for you yesterday! I handled goat cheese! If you don't accept my apology, I'll—I'll—" His eyebrows lifted into a peak. "I'll stay away from the wedding. Yeah, that way you won't have to see my stupid face. I'll even stay away from here so we won't run into each other ever again, because apparently you can't *stand* me." I felt my helplessness rising. If he argued back, that was one thing. But what could I say to silence? "Fine. Good-bye then. Forever!"

I was about to stomp out of the room in a fit when all of a sudden he reached out his right hand to my dad's phone and put the receiver to his ear. "Hello?" he said. I froze. Then he listened for a few seconds. "Mm-hmm. Mmmm. Okay." He hung up.

"Huh?" was the only thing I could say.

" 'Dawson's Creek' called," he commented. "They want their drama back."

What was that weird feeling on my chin? Oh, yes, my jaw hitting the industrial carpet. Before I could respond, Faris rolled his eyes and stood up. "Oh, come on," he said. "It's not that big a deal."

"Yes, it is. You should be upset," I insisted, though I nearly kicked myself for it afterward. I wasn't supposed to encourage him to be mad at me!

He shrugged. "I'll get over it. Okay, I was a little ticked. But hey, if Avril Lavigne had asked me out, I would've skipped out on that date too."

"A promise should be a promise, though. Doesn't matter who comes along after it's made."

He took a few steps closer. We were only an arm's length apart. "True." He nodded, his eyes never leaving mine. How was it that as awkward as he made me feel, I didn't at all want to run? "So if it happens again and, I don't know, Scotty or Kendrick asks you out—"

I managed to muster up a laugh, even though it sounded old and rusty. "Not gonna happen. Do you—do you still want to? I mean, you know. Go out sometime."

After a moment, he nodded. "Yeah," he said. His whisper sounded as hoarse as my laugh. "I want that to happen. A lot."

He held open his arms, but I made no move. We stood there. Simply stood there, until at least I made myself take the step forward and draw next to him. I rested my head on his shoulder, enjoying how real and strong and comfortable it felt. Finally his hands curled around my shoulder blades. His palms moved slowly up and down my spine. It felt good. When I made a little rumble of happiness, I felt a chuckle bubble up deep inside his chest. Hearing the source of his laughter made me wish that moment would last forever.

It couldn't, though. On the television I heard Aaron Grady, as tired and bored-sounding as ever, announcing what I'd waited for. "I've got to turn it up," I told Faris, grabbing the remote.

It was impossible to miss the look of disappointment on his face. "Yeah," he said flatly. "I know it's like, S.W.A.K. and all." Was it possible he was jealous? Really? Jealous over *me?*

". . . special guest performers today on the XT. They're on the road promoting their latest release, *Party on the S Dub*, and they're coming at ya live and unplugged . . . S.W.A.K.!"

The camera swung away from Aaron to four stools and mic stands bathed in a spotlight, where the boys in the band all sat. The audience applauded with enthusiasm. Somewhere in the back of my mind I wondered if my girls were managing to keep their cool. "You don't mind, do you?" I asked him.

He moved back to the desk and sat down with his arms crossed. "I guess I don't have a choice." The poor guy was upset again, I could tell.

On the screen, Antonio stood up, his microphone already in his hand. It was funny; even with all the boy band gear, I could see Eugene underneath. It was his street-talkin' alter ego who spoke, though. "Yo yo yo you, y'all, listen up. Sometimes it's hard to tell someone else what you're feelin' here." He pounded his chest. I moved back to lean on the desk beside Faris, who didn't budge.

"In the heart," Kendrick explained. I thought I heard someone in the audience let out an adoring groan.

"And sometimes, when you've done something wrong, or said something you shouldn't have, it's hard to open up and say you're sorry, y'all," said Antonio directly into the camera lens. "I'm sendin' out this one with a holler to my girl Hannah. Is Hannah out there, y'all?"

The cameras cut to the audience, where everyone was looking around. "I guess you'd rather be down in the studio," Faris said without a trace of amusement.

"Nuh-uh." I leaned in closer to him. "I'm exactly where I wanted to be." After a moment, his arm went around my shoulders again.

Antonio had given up on his search for me. "So this one's a dedication in the old school style, to Hannah's sister and her fiancé. They're gettin' married this week. Ain't that sweet? C'mon, give it up!"

As the applause died down, the band started snapping its fingers and broke into a ballad in perfect four-part harmony. "'Sor-ry is just not enough,'" they sang, quoting from the chorus, "'to say what you mean to meeeeee.'"

The camera suddenly cut to my sister, who looked absolutely horrified. She smiled at the camera in a panic. I could see a long finger jabbing down over her head, as if it was trying to point Molly out to the cameramen. Jasmine's, of course. Beside Molly stood Anas, unaware of the camera at all. He looked at her the way a man in love looks at a woman. When he reached out for her hand and she looked back at him, I could see that tears were making her eyes sparkle. She relaxed, and smiled.

I knew then that everything was going to work out.

". . . You're a rose on the stem, you're the moon at night, if you hold my hand, I will make it right. . . ." I turned down the sound again.

"That's what I wanted to see," I told Faris. "And if you'd still been in a snit, I kind of hoped the song might do some repair work for us too." I'd intended it to do triple duty in repairing multiple relationships.

"Yeah, that might've worked," he said, running his forefinger over my lips. When I looked up into his eyes, I wondered again what it would be like to kiss him.

And this time I didn't stop myself when our heads turned and our mouths sought each other.

It was several minutes later when I opened my eyes from his long, deep kisses. It felt like I'd drifted away into some blissful place between sleep and wakefulness, where nothing existed but pleasure—no sights, no sounds, nothing. It was hard to deny the noises coming from the outer office, though. When we pulled away, it felt like that awful moment on cold winter mornings when you've shucked your robe and run across the chilly room to hop into the shower. Yet I knew there would be more warmth to come, later. We smiled at each other and stepped away, our fingers lingering in one final squeeze.

"What's going on?" I asked. The outer office was mayhem. Everyone was there. Calvin was sitting on the sofa, talking. Dad was gesturing wildly at Fonzi. My friends were filing through the door. And over against the wall, holding hands, were Molly and Anas.

"Hannah!" I started to flinch when Molly made a beeline for me, dragging Anas behind her. Her hand flew out, and for a wild second I thought she was going to deck me. But then I found myself being choked in a tight, close embrace. "Oh, my God, that was the most special thing in the world you could have done for us! I love you so much!"

"I ove oo oo!" I gagged out, spots forming before my eyes. Finally she let me go. Fresh air had never tasted so sweet.

"Your mother and I are taking everyone out for pizza

tonight," Dad told me. Jasmine trotted over as well. My already watering eyes immediately felt worse when dazzled by so much pink patent pleather. "Feels like a celebration, right, sweetie? Kiss kiss?" He and Jasmine pecked each other on the lips while I averted my eyes.

"Your Antonio is *so sweet,*" Jasmine said to me, giving me a quick European kiss on both cheeks. "You should invite him as your date to the wedding,"

"Oh, Hannah, you *should!*" said Molly, squeezing my biceps in an Arnold Schwarzenegger grip of death. "Oh, my God," she said to Anas. "Can you imagine, my sister dating a *celebrity?*"

"Invite him!" called Mandy from behind Jasmine.

"Invite him!" squealed Taryn.

"Invite them all!" screamed Carrie. Her shout was so loud that everyone else in the room immediately fell quiet. Immediately she pretended nothing had happened. As if we were ever going to let her live this one down. Right.

It was only after the embarrassed pause that I saw everyone looking over their shoulders back to the chairs, where Calvin was talking to someone. Specifically, to Antonio. "Lady B!" Antonio said on seeing me, oblivious to the fuss. Apparently he hadn't heard Carrie. Was he maybe deaf? "So, did you like the dedication? Did I do it right?" He straightened up and spoke in his Eugene voice.

"That was great," I told him most sincerely. I looked around the room. Dad and Jasmine. Molly and Anas. Fonzi and Calvin. It was funny to think it, but I'd helped to forge little chains of love connecting them all.

"I'm sorry." I spoke not only to Molly and Jasmine

but to Antonio as well. "I think I already have a date to the wedding. I hope I do, anyway."

I looked back at Faris, still standing behind me. His lips twisted, as if he was in deep thought. Then they parted to show his teeth in a wide and gleaming smile. "You sure do," he said.

Molly looked disappointed, as if she'd been hoping for the social coup of the week, but Jasmine cried, "Oh!" and leaned over to hug us both. "We should find a nice girl for your little musical friend, though," she said confidentially. "What you two did was *so* sweet."

"You know, Jasmine," I said, shaking my head, "on the nice girl part, I'm thinking not so much. Know what I'm saying?"

"No, what's the dilly—I mean, why?" She thought about it a moment. *"Oh."* The word was pregnant with meaning. "Well. When you have artistic friends, that sort of thing's no problem. My friends know lots more nice boys than girls. Hmmmm."

I left her plotting and scheming to cross the room. "I don't mean to interrupt," I said to both Calvin and Antonio.

"Nah, child, Calvin's tellin' your friend here about how it was back in the day."

"Lady B!" It was strange. I recognized the excitement in Antonio's voice, but I couldn't quite place it. "You never told me you knew Calvin Desburne!"

"Aw, shucks, boy." Calvin made a face, but I could tell he was secretly pleased.

"Calvin? I've known him forever," I said.

"Calvin Desburne?"

"Um, yeah?"

195

"Calvin!" Antonio said for emphasis. "Desburne! *By the Fireplace with Calvin Desburne!*"

That's when I nailed the tone. He talked about Calvin with the same excited reverence I once used to gush about S.W.A.K. He was practically jumping up and down with excitement. Antonio was a fan boy! That was too much! "I know," I told him, totally calm and cool. "You should get him to cut a track with you guys." It was a spontaneous suggestion that I only made as a joke, but the minute it was out of my mouth, I realized it wasn't a half-bad idea.

"Child, get out of here," said Calvin. I could tell he was pleased as well, but too shy to admit it.

"Aw, yeah," said Antonio, jittery with joy. "Aw, yeah! Calvin Desburne with S.W.A.K.? That would be like, that would be like . . . !"

I never found out what that would be like. I had turned around to look back at Faris. When I saw that goofily adorable face across the room, his eyes following me, I wanted nothing more than to add another link to my chain—a link connecting him to me.

You know, I have the weirdest friends and family in the world. I knew in my heart that within days, if not hours, we'd all be squabbling and bickering again, then making up and moving on with our lives, only to do it all over again later. Right at that moment, though, our futures seemed bright and clear. Chains of love hung between us all at that moment. I could feel them, tangible as steel. We had enough love to contain all of Manhattan.

Epilogue

"Okay. Crunch time," said Taryn from her comfy nest on my bed. "How's it going?"

Although Carrie had nearly blackened her own eye in the mass scramble to grab Molly's bouquet the day before, it had been Fonzi who'd ended up scrambling away with the grand floral prize. In a single private moment toward the end of the wedding reception, Fonzi had given me a single yellow rose from the bunch. It lay on the floor right above my open notebook, its petals creamy and smooth. "I'm starting, I'm starting," I told her. It was no lie, either. My pen twitched in my fingers, ready to go.

"Does the word *deadline* not mean a thing to you?" she barked.

"Hey, chill. I've got it under control. You're supposed to be here for support, not to yell at me," I reminded her. "You know, best friend stuff?"

"I'm trying. Aren't you worried that you've only got a week left?" she asked.

"Nope, not at all." The first sheet in my notebook awaited its first marks.

Taryn didn't sound so certain. "What are you going to do?"

"You'll see."

CHAPTER ONE

boy (n) 1: a young male person 2: a junior version of the mature male, lacking the sophistication of the grown adult. As a species, they are frequently prone to . . .

"Prone to what?" I asked. Usually I love the first blank page in a notebook, when it's still clean and white and waiting to be filled with thoughts. I'd only captured thirty words on paper, though. Two of them were the chapter heading. I was pretty sure they would not count. Four thousand, nine hundred and seventy to go, and word number thirty-one simply wasn't coming to mind.

I was in a world of hurt.

I knew exactly what I was going to do. I would write about what I knew.

At long last, I'd finally be getting real.